Befor *Magic* *or*

The *Before* Series
Book 2

Michelle Deerwester-Dalrymple

Imprint: Independently published

This book is a work of fiction. Names, dates, places, and events are products of the author's imagination or used factiously. Any similarity or resemblance to any person living or dead, place, or event is purely coincidental.

Author's Note:

This book is not a traditional romance. Instead of steamy romance, these fairy tale reads are a bit darker and follows the depths of humanity in the lives of our favorite villains and characters before their infamous stories. Please be ready for something a bit darker, not steamy, and perhaps not the happy, fairy tale ending we are used to!

If you love this book, be sure to leave a review! Reviews are life blood for authors, and I appreciate every review I receive!

Love what you read? Want more from Michelle? Click the image below to receive Gavin, the free Glen Highland Romance short ebook, free books, updates, and more in your inbox. Go here:

https://linktr.ee/mddalrympleauthor

Before the Magic Mirror

Table of Contents

Before the Magic Mirror

Sometimes we must be patient for our fairy tale ending.

Before the Magic Mirror

Chapter One

THE PRINCE HELD *my* hand and poured honey-sweet compliments into *my* ear. *Mine.* What young woman was ever as fortunate as I? None.

The Christmas ball at the Prince-Bishop's Seta Castle in Valais, Switzerland, was pulled from an exquisite holiday dream. Sheer ruby-red fabric swathed the spruce wood rafters in long loops which were trimmed with evergreen and holly berry boughs. Dyed red and green candles burned from every sconce and cut crystal candle holder in the hall, and

9

the wax had been scented with pine and cinnamon. Combined with the rich aromas of the buffet — platters of Christmas hams, bowls dripping with cheesy scalloped potatoes, and plates overflowing with spicy walnut cake, Grittibänz cookies, and Lebkuchen gingerbread — the holiday scents of the hall created a distinctively festive air. The whole scene was magical. How could something wonderful not happen this night?

Women and men in brightly-colored gowns and surcoats milled about the food table, like colorful ornaments and ribbon attached to pine trees for the season. Laughter and chatter filled the room and competed with the music of the royal quartet, whose minuet and waltzes compelled even the least prolific dancer to find a partner on the floor.

When I entered the royal hall with my parents, my eyes looked everywhere at once. There was too much to take in. The music, the lights, the scents, the dresses, the foods! I was certain I had been just as captivated the year before. As I wasn't of age, I'd been stuck with the children in the lower salon. This year was my year, as a Baron's daughter, to join the real Christmas party and be a part of the festivities.

I joined my parents at the edge of the red carpet that led to the center of the hall between the buffet and the dancers. Stepping up next to my parents, I blushed in a warm rush as much of the chaotic chatter in the hall fell away to a quieter din.

I knew the image I presented — my brazen red silk gown clung to my body invitingly, with red and white ribbons encrusted with crystals woven into my chestnut hair. The red seemed even bolder against my milky white skin and silver-gray eyes. Oh, my own image in my small bedroom mirror had shown me what a vision I was! I was like a Christmas Princess, all red and white, and now, as I glided into the royal hall, I garnered the attention of everyone present. It was at once breathtaking and exhilarating.

We were announced amid the cluster of other barons and families of import — the Von Rushses, the Von Scuffers, the Boscherts, and Odermatts who crowded the gleaming hall. Farther up on the raised dais, the Prince-Bishop, the king of our canton, sat in his royal glory. His rich black hair was heavily salted with white, and it curled to his shoulders where it brushed his bright red velvet cape. Seated on the dais with him were royalty from other cantons, his refined wife, Queen Gerta, and his son, Werner, the future Prince-Bishop.

To say Prince Werner Von Erlach was coveted by all young women in Valais canton, and all the surrounding cantons, was a gross understatement. He was a taller, more muscular version of his father. Still lean but packed with solid muscle borne of horsemanship and outdoor athletics. His dark hair

11

was raven-black, the black of a night without the moon, or of a lake in the nighttime shadows. Wavy and with a rich sheen under the candlelight, it swept back from the strong features of his face and was tied with a white ribbon at the back of his neck. His surcoat, more burgundy than bright red, flattered his lighter eyes that were the color of candlelight themselves. He looked like a consummate Christmas prince.

How were we not designed for each other?

My father took my mother's elbow in one hand and my elbow in the other, and stood patiently on the carpet, awaiting our announcement.

"My king, may I present Baron Von Gueff, his wife Baroness Von Gueff, and his daughter, Adalee Von Gueff."

My father bowed as far as he could over his portly belly, and my mother and I curtsied in tandem. After a mild applause from the crowd, we pressed forward to the end of the carpet. My mother remained by my side, greeting other nobles with a wide smile, as my father made his way to the buffet. Of course, he would. He only attended these events for the food.

I was leaning into a beautiful and buxom woman to better hear her, having missed the introduction by my mother, when a movement caught my attention. I looked over her head to find the Christmas Prince moving from the dais to join the dancers on the floor. His champagne eyes were bright and eager and focused on me.

That night, Werner saw me, cut through the crowd of eager subjects, party attendees, and besotted young women, and came straight for me. He saw me and me alone. My heart had fluttered like a newly-birthed butterfly when he grasped my hand in his large, warm fingers. The royal musicians had just struck up a leisurely waltz.

"May I have this dance?" he asked, his voice just as enchanting as the rest of him.

How could I say no? I nodded, my cheeks and bare chest warming, flushed under the Prince's attentions and the jealous gaze of the other young women in the hall. And when he spun me in the steps of the dance, his arms were strong and his eyes sparking. Maybe this night was an exquisite Christmas dream.

For the rest of the night, under the magically incandescent light of the crystal chandeliers, he remained by my side. He caressed my hand and filled my ears with the most romantic of words. I fairly swooned.

I'd hated leaving that night, and when he promised to call on me and kissed my hand before I departed, right on the same spot he'd caressed, I was smitten.

I don't think my feet touched the ground the entire way home.

I didn't tell anyone but my grandmother that I wanted a love spell for him the very next day. My heart had burned with fire for Werner since that first look at the Christmas soirée. The air was frigid, and we were both wrapped in woolen shawls against the chill that permeated my Grandmother's drafty cottage. Mother had offered her chambers in the manse, but Grandmother rejected them, preferring the privacy of her quaint cottage.

When I poured my girlish desires into my grandmother's patient ear the next day, she had smiled, crinkling her already wrinkled gray eyes, and reached into her cupboard for several leather satchels and a pestle. She'd made potions and spells for me in the past, trivial, childish spells to indulge a spoiled little girl, and still I'd clung to the stool, mesmerized as her thin, bowed body worked earnestly, mixing the herbs and petals into a bowl, grinding it with the pestle, then reaching a gnarled hand to me.

"Hold still, Adalee," she'd commanded in her surprisingly strong voice and plucked a single hair from my head.

"Ow!" I'd yelped as she smiled and added my hair to the bowl, grinding it in with the rest. Then she had poured the mixture into a fresh satchel.

"The next time you see your man, pour this in his drink. 'Twill make him fall in love with you.

At the time, I didn't take the proffered satchel, not at first.

"Grandmother, he's a prince! What would he do with the likes of me? 'Tis not like we might wed or anything."

She had waggled her finger at me and pushed the satchel into my hand. "In that, you are wrong. Most magic is nothing more than putting your desires out into the universe. These trappings, they help make it real. You are the stunningly beautiful daughter of a wealthy baron. He already expressed an interest last night. The prince could do no better than to wed you."

I'd dropped my gaze, smiling with pride at my grandmother's boasts. She was my grandmother, so she had to say it, but her words were the sweetest music to my ears. I had always been the apple of her eye, the child she'd wished to have in a daughter, and that made me love her all the more. `

In the end, I had grasped the satchel and tucked it into my bodice. Then I added it to his wine the next time he and his father visited our manse.

And Werner kissed me for the first time under the stars later that night. The stars winked at me as the light touch of his lips caressed mine, as though the universe approved of my choice.

Did the love potion help? Maybe.

I wasn't about to doubt the magic my grandmother knew. She claimed not to be a witch, yet her magic always seemed to work.

And work it did. I may have fretted and worried about Grandmother's magic, but as usual, her skills were sound.

Four months later, our salon was crowded, full of colorful gowns and smiling faces and rich flaxen wine. I cut my eyes to Werner, hoping he saw my silvery blue gaze. One smile from him was all I needed to make it through this soirée.

My mother had gone overboard with the engagement party, decorating with draping ivory damask and inviting the creme de la creme of our demesne to our home. Everyone from neighboring barons to our solicitor Hans Von Ruchse attended, showering Werner and me with gifts. Werner's birthright as the future Prince-Bishop did matter when it came to gift giving. Every gift we'd received had been ornate and expensive. My favorite engagement gift was a bathing set with an embroidered towel meant for Werner and I to bathe together. I had flushed with warmth as I opened the velvet cloth bag to expose the exquisite set, as its use was obvious, but it only made me more excited about my upcoming nuptials.

My father might have only been a baron, but he was a wealthy one, and the king's coffers couldn't pass up the rich dowry that came with the hand of the baron's only child. Wealthy nobility outweighed royalty in my case.

The fact that Werner and I were wildly in love and would have married anyway, fat purse or no, made the match all the better.

Werner caught my gaze and his own glance, as intoxicating as the wine we were drinking and just as golden, made my heart skip a beat. His beguiling eyes crinkled in the corners, and I knew he was smiling at me. How had I managed to find this man, my heart, my soulmate, out of all the men in this world? He stood a scant few inches taller than me, which pleased me to no end. As a taller woman, I fretted I would be fettered to a man who barely reached my chin. My mother had commented on it more than once, much to my disdain. Instead, I had landed this black-haired prince. Even amid the chaos of all these people, my attention focused on this one man and one man only.

My mother kept raising her embellished goblet to us, as did the king. My father was too busy eating the rich breads that accompanied our pheasant dinner, his short arms struggling to reach around his portly belly. But even my father's desire to eat rather than celebrate didn't dampen my spirits. I just needed my mother to set her goblet down already, so I might sneak out the back and hide in the garden shadows with this man who'd been crafted from my dreams.

I didn't tell anyone but my grandmother that I had tried out a love spell on him. My heart had burned with fire for Werner since I'd first met him. He was my future, and I was more than ready to walk into it with him.

As the night wore on, the attendees grew more interested in their drinks and food and laughter. My father had even managed to push his plate away, and his belly jiggled like a bowl of marmalade as he laughed with the current Prince-Bishop at some joke or piece of canton gossip. With everyone's attention focused elsewhere, I leapt at the opportunity.

I lifted my embellished, black, velvet lined cape, slipped the hood over my finely coiffed russet locks, and snuck out through the kitchens. Olga, the kitchen matron, tipped her head and pretended not to see me as I stepped out the door into the dark, dew-kissed gardens.

Hopefully, the flowers weren't going to have the only kisses that night.

The gardens were quiet, with only the gentle rustle of the wind in the trees, carrying on it the damp scents of late spring — hyacinth and grass and edelweiss. All of earth's creatures slept, leaving the privacy of the gardens to my prince and me.

My prince didn't disappoint. He stepped from the side of the manse, his rich burgundy surcoat blending into the shadows. With only a single torchlight in an iron sconce by the kitchen door, deep shadows hid the rest of the gardens. And Werner guided me into them, away from any potential prying eyes.

"Adalee, my love, my silver-eyed beauty. I thought I might wither away if I had to suffer my father's raucous stories one more time. I came to this event to be with you, and we have to sneak away for that to happen." He kissed my palm as if to confirm his affections. How my heart fluttered at the gentle press of his full lips!

I reached my hand to his fair face, his golden eyes glimmering like the firelight, his jaw soft, shaved clean of any hair. His face was that of a lad's, though he was a full grown man preparing to take over as king after his father.

"You are not to blame. Nor your father. If anything, I was certain my ears would bleed if my mother tried to hoist her goblet over my father's head again."

The heady rumbling of his laughter vibrated in my chest. Had any man's laugh been such a gift from the angels? No, none. Only my Werner.

He pressed his tender lips to mine, claiming me, and his bold hands traced the curves of my long body over the thick, bronzed brocade of my gown. Such an intimate touch! I wanted to melt into him, unite with him right there in the gardens! How would I wait until our wedding day? I burned for him, my insides consumed into ash.

I lifted my head to inhale the clean night air and clear my head. Werner caught himself and stepped away. His hands, however, yet held mine, pulsing with warmth and chasing away any lingering chill of the evening. Not that I felt any of it, his forward attentions igniting a fire deep in my belly.

"My apologies, my love. I am far too forward. You are a refined lady and deserve to be treated as such. It's just so hard for me to keep my hands off you, to —"

His hands clenched against mine as he spoke, as if the passion and intensity surging inside him came through his fingertips.

"No, not your fault. I, too, dread the days until we can be wed. Each will linger far too long. I crave you as much as you crave me, my prince."

He risked another step, closing the gap between us. Placing a quick, chaste kiss on my forehead, he inhaled as well, his chest brushing against mine, and moved backward. Then he turned my hand over and kissed the palm again, and my legs quivered.

"Only a few short weeks, and it shall be true. I can wait that long." He kissed my hand again. "I would wait a lifetime for you."

Before the Magic Mirror

Before the Magic Mirror

Before the Magic Mirror

Chapter Two

I ROSE FAR too late the following day — the sun glared brightly and welcoming in the heavens. While it pained my sleepy eyes, I felt as though it shone just for me. To celebrate Werner and me and our profound love. Had any couple in history loved this much? Romeo and Juliet, Paris and Helen, their love was naught compared to the unbridled passion Werner and I shared.

Or rather, a bridled passion that I desperately awaited to *become* unbridled. If his kiss on my lips made my entire body melt, what would his kisses do on my skin once we were wed? My fantasies paled in comparison to that anticipated moment.

I rose from my plush, embroidered quilt and crisp counterpane and glanced around my bed chamber. The manse was quiet, still, and I wondered where everyone was this day. Had everyone over imbibed and still abed? Even the servants? Had they snuck drinks whilst the baron and baroness were otherwise occupied? It had happened before. Baron Von Gueff's servants were nearly as gluttonous as the Baron himself. And everyone had celebrated long into the night. I doubted I'd see mother rise before noon.

"Emma, where are you? Am I too late for breakfast?" I called out as I pulled my soft, edelweiss-stitched bed gown from the bedstead and tied it over my shift.

Usually, my breakfast sat atop my engraved table by the window if I woke late. Everything in my room was like that table, engraved and refined and plush — a chambers fit for a queen. *Well, almost a queen,* I giggled to myself.

This morn, only my loose papers and quill sat atop the tabletop. Where was breakfast? Where was Emma?

Sliding a pair of slippers onto my feet, I rose quickly, departed my chambers and headed down the stairs. I hadn't rounded the whitewashed wall yet when I heard my mother and father whispering with someone else — a man with a gruff voice. Something inside me demanded I wait, not turn the corner yet, and listen to the words that had cast a pall on my otherwise bright morning. I leaned against the wall, the chill of the stone seeping through my bed gown and shift. That chill drove through my skin to my spine.

"Milord, we can try to send an emissary to speak on your behalf, or better, you go yourself, but I don't see any way around this. The current Prince-Bishop has made his decision, as he claims, for the good of the canton."

The voice was of my father's solicitor, Hans Von Ruchse, who'd drunk more than his fair share of apricot brandy the night before. He should still be abed with an aching head and sour stomach, not here in our salon, which meant that whatever business he had was serious. Very serious. The chill became cold, and I gathered my bed robe tightly around my neck. My grandmother had told me that I was like her, full of magic and premonition, and though I hesitated to use any of it (*oh, how I lacked Grandmother's self-confidence*), right now I believed her. Because I had a sinking sensation that this *decision* they discussed concerned me.

Why else would the house be so hushed?

"Adalee, what are you doing by the stairs?" Emma's squeaky voice surprised me, and I spun around.

Her hands clutched a tray covered with fruit and eggs. My delayed breakfast? The luscious purple berries called out to me, and normally, I would have scooped a handful and relished their sweetness. But this morning, my stomach knotted and the sight of food made my gorge rise.

"Emma, do you know why the solicitor is here?" I asked in a hushed voice.

Emma dropped her eyes to the tray. "I'm not sure, but it must be dire if Von Ruchse is in attendance."

She's lying. That thought lit my brain up like the sun as I studied her. Her shoulders under her lawn maid's outfit were tight, and she kept shifting her gaze. She did know, and if she feared speaking the words, then it must be something very dire.

"Adalee, is that you? Please join us in the salon."

My mother's voice warbled, almost weeping, and I froze where I stood. I didn't want to hear it. If I didn't hear what the solicitor had to say, then it wouldn't be real.

"Adalee, please. I see your bed gown." My mother wouldn't let me escape.

With heavy feet, I dragged myself into the lushly decorated salon and perched on the edge of a velvet-covered beige wing chair. I kept my head lowered, my wild, darkly russet locks forming a curtain, a barrier, against whatever my mother was going to say. I didn't want to look at them, not my mother's watery blue eyes or my father's soft jowls.

"Adalee," my father began, "we have some news."

Then he paused, and I couldn't tell if he was sad or angry. I usually read my father so well, like my favorite book. Today, however . . .

"We've had some news," the solicitor picked up where her father's faltering voice hesitated. "The canton of Uli has encountered some sad events. A disease has spread across their lands. The daughter of their Prince-Bishop, the princess Berta, lost her betrothed last month. Her father recently reached out to our Prince-Bishop and offered her hand to his son as a way to form an alliance in these uneasy times."

No! He's lying! I snapped my head up. "What do you mean? My Prince Werner? But he's betrothed to me. She can't marry my betrothed."

Hans shared a disconcerting look with my mother and father, and I knew before he spoke what horrendous news he was bound to share.

"No," I said, preempting him. "No, no, no. I'm betrothed to Werner. We have a contract! Father—" I flashed my eyes to my father as panic bubbled under my skin and fevered my brain.

27

He shook his head with slow despair.

"Not quite," the solicitor said, his voice slow and precise. "The Prince-Bishop and your father were finalizing the contract. Nothing yet has been signed."

"You didn't sign it?"

I was falling. The earth under my feet had disappeared, and I was tumbling into the nether. This was *impossible*! We'd spent months arranging this betrothal! Now it wouldn't happen because they had delayed in signing? No, not *my* Werner! Wed to another? Surely he would protest! My prince was not a weakling to bow to the whims of his father — was he?

Wiping my tears from my eyes, I launched myself to my father and knelt before him. I rested my head on his paunchy lap and sobbed out my anguish. He placed a doughy hand on my hair.

"Please, Father! Please! Make the Prince-Bishop see sensibly. Werner and I love each other! Werner is my soulmate. We've made our own vows to each other! Please, don't do this!"

I'd heard the phrase *heartbreak* before, but thought it just a word, not a real event. A heart couldn't actually break. But it was real. My heart was shattering as I knelt on the floor of my father's salon, splintering into thousands of pieces as though it were glass. And like glass, each sharp edge cut me deeper, a thousand knives in my chest at once.

How did one live with such pain? How could I?

Father's hand moved to cup my head, the most fatherly gesture I'd had from him since I was a child. "I'm sorry, my lovey. It's not up to me. The Prince-Bishop is the king, and he has spoken."

The king of Valais canton had decided. It was done. His son, my betrothed, would marry someone else, and I would be alone, without my prince, without my future husband, without my heart.

"I hate you!" I shouted at my father as I jumped up and pounded my foot against the stone floor as if I were a toddler and not a young woman ready to wed. "I hate you all for doing this to me!"

Then I ran. I ran for the only place that would welcome me.

Grandmother's decrepit house was at the edge of the manse property. Fraying roof thatch, a lopsided window, a low narrow door that I had to duck under to enter. Small but perfectly suited for my quirky, sage grandmother, and it seemed as old as she was.

I slammed my fists into her wooden door over and over until splinters riddled my hands. I didn't care. No pain could outweigh the horrific pain of losing Werner to that, *that* princess! The door swung open and my grandmother looked up her sharp nose at me — I had inherited that sharp nose. I had inherited so much from her, it endeared her to me all the more. Only she would help me now.

"Adalee! What ails you? And why are you here in your bed gown?" She threw the door open wide and ushered me into her humble home as she looked me over.

"Grandmother," I sobbed, wiping my eyes with my sleeve, "it's over! Werner has been betrothed to another!"

She shook her head. "No, surely you are mistaken," she said as she patted my hand. "Here, have some tea, and tell me all about it."

Grandmother always made me feel better, and she endeavored to do that now. But nothing would make me feel better this time. Not Grandmother's cottage, not tea. My life was over.

I poured my misery out to my grandmother like she poured the tea. She sat across from me, silent, studying on my misery as she picked the wood splinters from my pale skin with her silver tweezers. When no more words formed on my lips, she patted my hand again.

"Oh, my sweet, it's not the end of the world, though it might seem that way. I have a solution that might help you."

I sat up straight. "You have a potion or a spell that will bring Werner back to me?" I choked out. My heart leapt to my chest. Oh, that she did have such a spell! Surely a love token?

Grandmother pressed her creased lips together softly, then spoke in a low, caring voice. A softer voice than I ever recalled her using. "No, my sweet. Love potions and token are for those who are unfettered. But I have a solution that might help with your heartache. And something I think you're ready to see. Come."

She took my hand in her dry, wrinkled one and led me to the side of her hearth, where a unique square rock blended into the whitewashed wall. Grandmother pressed on the wall and it swung open behind the hearth.

I gaped at it. What was she showing me? A tunnel? She was ever the mystery.

"Grandmother, what's this?"

"Let me show you."

Gripping my hand tightly, she dragged me into the narrow dirt tunnel. The short distance was reinforced with wood buttresses that made the passageway feel even more constricted. Grandmother carried no torch, but she didn't need one. She knew the way to go as though she could see in the pitch black. After several steps, we arrived at a wood panel door that she pushed inward to expose a stone-walled room lit with torches.

My eyes went wide with awe, and my mouth was agape. What *was* this place?

Shelves covered two of the walls and held collections of jars, pots, sachets, books, bowls, and what appeared to be bones. *Bones?* The far wall hosted a wide, open hearth with an iron hook inside that held a cauldron. A raven cawed at us from inside a cage that hung over a large table cluttered in utter disarray. Spilled herbs, potions, pots, wooden spoons, and a bronze book stand that held an ancient looking open book. The entire room was bathed in an air of dust and mystery.

"What is this, Grandmother?" Awe filled my voice.

Grandmother stood with her hands on her hips, pride sparkling in her watery gray eyes. She looked around the room, assessing it.

"My cellar. My *atelier*. I can access it from my croft using that tunnel, or if you look at the stone next to the hearth, a stone stairway blends in with the wall and leads to the wine cellar below the manse. This is another level below, one only I, and your grandfather, God rest his soul, know about."

"Not even Father?" I asked as I peeked at the miscellany of items on the shelves. What *was* all this? I have never been so intrigued by anything in all my life.

"Nope. I hid it from him. Now only you and I know about my cellar."

"What is all this, though? What are these things? This book is older than the manse." I reached out to touch it, then withdrew my hand, afraid it would disintegrate under my fingers.

"You've seen me dabble with my potions and tokens. This is where some of the larger dabbling takes place."

"Larger dabbling?"

Grandmother's thin smile widened. "You don't think it was your father's brilliance that brought him his wealth and power, do you? Or brought his doughy body a woman as beautiful as your mother, who then produced an incomparable beauty such as yourself?"

I'm sure my jaw still hung open. Unladylike, my mother would chastise me. Grandmother was the sort who didn't put any measure into ladylike standards or constructs. She let me gape as long as I desired.

"No, that was all me. Well, me and my spells."

I clutched my bed robe to my neck. "Spells? Like a witch?" My voice gasped in an incredulous whisper.

Grandmother nodded, her thin smile more of a grin on her wizened face. *She's enjoying this!*

"A good witch, not really a witch as you think. I'd never use my spells for evil."

I traced my finger along the worn-smooth wood of the table, wondering if I believed her. What witch didn't use her spells for her own advancement, good or evil? And would Grandmother tell me if she did? No, I didn't believe she would.

"So, what now? Are you going to use a spell so I can get Werner back?"

Getting him back would heal that heartache. And that was the option I'd push for, if I could.

"No, I told you we can't do that. That would make us trek into some very dark, black magic, magic I won't dare use. However, as promised, I can try to heal your heartache. Do you want me to try?"

Get rid of this pain? I would do anything for that. If I couldn't have Werner, then the pain wasn't worth it. "Yes, of course!"

Grandmother stood in front of me, her smile gone from her pale, pinched face. "I have to warn you, my sweet, that spells and potions don't always work the ways we like. This might not work at all, or if it does, it might work too well, and harden your heart completely." She grasped both of my hands in hers, and her eyes bored into mine. "Are you willing to risk that?"

I was sure she exaggerated. And her other potions had always worked as she'd said — surely this one would work as well. I nodded, eager for her to start.

"I am. What do I need to do?"

Grandmother pursed her lips, then turned me toward the table. "Now is as good a time as any to start."

"Start what?"

"Start your training. Since you aren't getting married right away, you'll work with me every day, learning how to cast your own spells. I don't want this trait to die with me."

"Grandmother," I said sharply, dismissing her, "don't say such a thing."

"Oh, my sweet, my time will come soon enough, but we have time to train you. You could become an even greater spell caster than I am, I believe. So, we will start with your heartbreak potion. It's in my book, here."

Grandmother flipped the crumbly paper open to the correct page, and the dark text seemed to dance on the parchment.

Greater than Grandmother? A witch? My mind reeled from all I'd learned in the past day. I didn't believe her, but her words yet tickled my ears with such opportunity. And she was right — it would give me something to do with myself. Better than sitting around, pining for Werner.

I leaned in, watching her and listening attentively as she pulled down pots and jars, extracted strange items (eye of crow?), and mixed herbs. When she was done, she stepped to her hidden staircase and disappeared. When she returned, she held a bottle of

fine Rouen wine in her hand. She popped the cork
with an archaic-looking extractor device, then poured
a nearby goblet half full. With her gnarled hand, she
sprinkled the crumbly mixture into the wine and
offered the heavy goblet to me.

"Drink, and your heart will harden against
Werner. You will no longer crave his love, his touch,
or anything from the man. But remember, this won't
change ever, so if he can return to you some way, you
won't love him the way you did before you drank."

Won't love him again? That was fine for me.
Because of Berta, he was lost to me forever, anyway.

I grabbed the goblet, gave my grandmother a
ferocious look, then put the drink to my lips and
swallowed the sour wine.

I thought I'd feel something, a twinge in my
chest of my heart hardening, a throbbing in my head
of my mind shielding against any loving feelings
toward Werner. Something . . .

But nothing. Grandmother wasn't looking at
me — she was studying her book with an intensity I
hadn't seen on her before.

"It didn't work, Grandmother. I still feel the
same."

"Oh, my sweet," she said as she took the goblet from me without looking. "It will take some time. You just watch."

She set the goblet on the table, her eyes never leaving that book. I stood behind her, reading from it over her shoulder.

The strangely shimmering words danced under her gaze. Grandmother's crooked finger traced the lines of the potion as she read. I followed her finger, reading the strange commands and recipes.

"What's this spell for, Grandmother? And what is all this? Why are you showing me your secret? It can't be just to learn this potion and drink it."

Her finger in the book paused. I was right – there was something more to Grandmother's intentions.

"Your training. I'm old, sweet, I told you that."

"Not that old, Grandmother," I countered.

"Yes, that old. I was old when you were born, but when you came squalling from your mother's womb, I was relieved. I finally had the girl I needed."

I tried not to stiffen — this was my grandmother, not someone I should fear. Why did her words send a shiver down my spine?

"You needed for what?" I kept my voice as level as I could as I gazed down my nose at her. She wasn't serious about the training she'd mentioned. Was she?

She spun around and placed a wrinkly hand on my face. She appeared to have aged in the time we were in the cellar.

"You are so beautiful, my sweet. You know that? Your sharp cheekbones, your ethereal eyes, your ruby lips and milky skin. I used to be as beautiful, but I gave it up when you were born. Instead of pouring my efforts into me, I poured them into you. I wanted you to be the most beautiful, so the whole world would fall at your feet. That didn't end the way I'd expected. Now it's time for something more. I told you. To begin your own training so these skills don't end with me."

Goose pimples covered my skin. I suddenly didn't want her hand on my face. This woman who had loved me more than anything now frightened me.

"A woman needs more than her looks. You will have yours for a long time yet, I've made certain of that. And now it's time for something more. You already know so much about my potions, having watched me since you were a girl, and you are far too clever for a woman, so your training should be easy."

"My training?" I was still so dubious, so disbelieving. It was all so impossible!

She moved her hand from my face and trailed it down my arm, taking my hand. "Yes. You will be even better than I at making spells. This cellar will become yours, and the world will quiver at your feet. Are you ready for that much power?"

I forget about everything else — my bed gown, my slippered feet, my incompetent parents, my love for Werner — these concerns fell to the side as I spun my gaze around this dark, mysterious cellar. She *was* a witch. Grandmother wouldn't admit it, wouldn't use the word, but even a fool could see it. And she was offering all of this power of her magical arts to me. All I had to do was accept it.

Could I do that? Take in this power and use it responsibly?

I touched my chest. I'd already used her potions and tokens, why not learn how to create them? Oh, Grandmother knew me too well.

"Yes," I told her.

And her potion must have worked. I didn't think on Werner for the rest of the day.

Before the Magic Mirror

Chapter Three

EVERY DAY, I grabbed my hooded cloak and rushed to the cellar, ready to learn from my grandmother. Her patience knew no bounds as she showed me the different herbals, the importance of saying the complicated words, and the nuances among the spells. My parents tried to question me, my mother's suspicious eyes following me as I swept out the door. I didn't answer — what right did they have to the inner workings of my mind when it was their fault I'd lost Werner?

I wasn't the best student. Poor Grandmother. She was so kind, so patient with me. She started me on the easiest potions – ones where, if I made a mistake, the outcome wasn't too dire.

"What types of spells do you want to try?" She lifted a gnarled hand toward her precious black book. "The more invested you are in the spell and its outcome, the better chance it will have of working. So which one?"

Grandmother stepped to the side, giving me the chance to peruse her text. The filmy paper threatened to dissolve at the slightest touch, so I kept my fingers light. A list of potion types was handwritten in large scrawl at the front of the book, so I started there.

Love, of course, was listed first. I scoffed and moved my finger down.

Wealth. Well, useful, but right now, wealth wasn't a concern for my family. The Baron, my father, was renowned for his fortune.

Happiness, Harmony, the Earth (whatever that meant).

Health.

My mind flicked to my father and his generous belly that demanded too much of his buttons. That heaviness had begun to extend to his face, his hands, and his breathing. I'd seen my mother's face tighten whenever he took an extra slice of Swiss nut cake. Dripping and sweet with raspberry and walnuts, even I'd snuck a second slice more than once when the baker made it. But then, I didn't have a belly like my father. Now that I thought on it — we hadn't had nut cake in a long time.

I wasn't the only one worried about my father. I cut a glance at Grandmother. Was she worried about him as well? If so, she didn't show it.

"Health," I said, pointing to the page. "What health potions are there?"

"Good choice. If you do something wrong, there's just no effect. If you do it right, then one's health improves."

"What about if I messed up on another spell? Like Happiness?"

A shadow crossed over the deep lines of Grandmother's face, then she smiled, and it disappeared.

"Not all, but some of the potions and spells, the darker ones, have negative effects if they go wrong. Not necessarily an opposite outcome, just a negative one." Then she patted my hand reassuringly. "I'll teach you well but expect to have some less-than-desired outcomes. This magic, 'tis not an exact practice."

I should have been more attentive to her statement, but the gentle smile on her face beguiled me, and I let it pass without another thought. My focus was on a health potion that might help my father.

Grandmother's fingertip trailed over the words in her book, and she grabbed my wrist with her bony hand to show me how to find each ingredient, how to measure out the correct amounts. Then her gnarly finger pointed to some faint words written under the recipe.

"Most potions are just potions. Spells and potions work together. So start by combining all these into this bowl."

It was an ordinary wooden bowl. I shrugged and did as she bid, and then she handed me a large metal spoon made for porridge and directed me to mix it all together. Once she nodded to approve my work, she handed me a short, fat, grubby-white candle.

"Light it and drip it into the pot. When the smoke of the flame rises above the bowl, chant the words printed here and think of your father."

Again, I did as she instructed. When I was done, I looked at her.

"What else?"

She shrugged one bony shoulder. "That's it, dearie. There's not much to most of these bright potions or spells if you know how to use them."

I glanced around the shadowy, chilly cellar. "Do you know how to do all these spells?" It seemed impossible that she'd read about, let alone used, each of these spells.

Grandmother giggled like a young girl. "No, not by half. But the information the books contain is valuable, and you never know when you're going to need a potion. While I might be able to make changes to the world, I can't begin to guess the future. Some potions and spells might give you a hint, but I've encountered nothing that will tell it to me outright."

Peering back into the bowl, I watched mesmerized until most of the smoke had disappeared.

"How do we know if it worked?"

Grandmother began setting her cellar to rights, sealing the jars and putting her beloved book on its shelf. She paused to smile weakly at me.

"We wait."

She'd said the same about the heartbreak potion. I pursed my lips.

I wasn't a patient woman.

One day I found the courage to ask Grandmother about the other book of spells and potions, the one whose pages were not as stained or worn as her more common book.

Her whole face tightened, and she slammed her hand on the pages.

"Why do you want to know about the black spells, Adalee?" she asked in a wavering voice.

I didn't have a decent answer. It just seemed that I should know as much as possible, and I told her so.

"Better that than I try on my own later and really make a muck of things."

Grandmother's blue eyes darkened so they appeared almost black, and her harrowing expression told me what she thought of those spells and potions. And what she thought of my answer. But to my surprise, she nodded.

"These spells can be powerful. And they often work better than then other spells. But they come at a cost."

"A cost?"

Grandmother's eyes studied me, her intense gaze roving over me as if she were evaluating me. Perchance she was. I stood tall, as if I might exude preparedness with my stance.

"All things come at a cost, girlie. Most of the time, we don't know we are paying that cost. Those costs come as payments in time or effort or heartache. But these spells, well, when they work, they demand a payment, and the recipient of the spell pays that cost almost immediately."

I tilted my head, trying to make sense of all she was telling me. Cost? Payments?

"I'm sorry, Grandmother. I don't understand."

"Black spells all have a cost. Do you recall the family that lost everything in that fire to the south years ago?"

Barely. I'd been so young, but I had scattered memories of gray smoke staining the skies and the acrid smell that hung in the air for days.

"Yes, I think so."

Grandmother's shoulders slumped, and she wrapped her thin arms around herself, as if she'd caught a sudden chill.

"The wife, she was devastated. Her family's livelihood gone, all their possessions consumed by the fire. A few animals, her husband, and their children were all that remained."

"But, that's good, right? That no one died in the fire?"

Grandmother clicked her tongue at me. "You come from wealth, dearie, and with that comes a measure of security. This woman had no food to feed her babes, no roof over her head, no place to keep her beasts. The fire took their security. So she came to me."

"But wouldn't a spell or potion for wealth come from this book?" I pointed at the grubby, worn pages of her main book she kept out daily. Grandmother shook her head.

"Oh, she wanted her home restored. That's where we started. But the fire, it hadn't been an accident. Her husband had gotten into a drunken fight at the tavern the night before, gambling, and he'd won a fair bit of coin. The man who'd lost wasn't a virtuous man by any means, and he was the one who'd set the house and barns ablaze."

I gasped and slapped my hand to my mouth. Who would do such a vicious act? The family could have perished! And for some coin? A lost wager?

Grandmother patted my knee. "You will learn, dearie, that most people are kind. But not all. Be wary of those who might not be."

"What happened to the man who set the house on fire?" I asked in a hoarse whisper. I wanted desperately to know, but at the same time, my chest shook in fear at the harrowing tale Grandmother was about to share.

"The wife, she wanted her vengeance taken out in kind. So she asked, nay, demanded that I set a spell against him, a punishment spell. There was no hard proof it was this man who set the fire, but rumors abounded."

"And you did it? The black spell?"

Grandmother hung her head. "I've done them in the past, a few, and I'm not proud, but nothing, nothing like this."

"What happened?" I had leaned in close to her beautifully wrinkled face, hungry to hear the rest.

48

"I did it. She asked that the man be punished and lose everything he owned. Well, he did. But then he lost his mind to drink and got lost in the wood in the winter, froze to death, leaving behind a wife and daughter."

This time, both my hands clapped over my mouth. He'd died? Oh, that payment was far too dear. Yet, the cost was paid by the man, not the person who requested the spell . . . Did that make a difference?

Grandmother must have noted the confusion on my face. "Oh, that wasn't the cost. That was just the beginning of a black spell taking its toll. The woman, she fell sick, but recovered. Only, while she was ill, she couldn't help care for their animals, and all their stock died that winter as well."

Grandmother pressed toward me so her nose brushed against my hands clamped over my mouth. "That was the cost. The black spell had demanded too much, and I've regretted it ever since. Nor have I cast a black spell in all this time. I couldn't bring myself to do it again. The ramifications took their toll on me."

Her tale complete, she sat back, exhaled in a long, quivering breath, then rose to fiddle with the jars on a shelf.

"Then why do you keep the books?" I dared to ask.

Grandmother reached on her tippy-toes to pat the books into place, as if securing them high and tucked away.

"My grandmother trained me, and she handed down the books. They are old, ancient even, and I fear them falling into the wrong hands. Here, I can keep them safe and tucked away." Settling back down on her feet, she resumed her work at the table. "Black spells are powerful, effective, and costly, Adalee. And every time, every single time, remember that the cost will always be far too dear. So we stick to the white magic, my dearie."

I didn't reply, yet I nodded at her backside. I'd remember, I vowed silently.

I was lost in the wonders of Grandmother's cellar on the day Werner wed a pasty-faced, black-haired woman. My parents forced me to attend the pageant prior the wedding. The confetti and ribbons, the music and cheering, it all made me sick, the bile at the back of my throat choking me. I clenched my stomach with my hands, wrapping my fingers in the folds of my bright blue skirts. My mother inquired about my health, and my eyes spoke what my mouth didn't. Thankfully, they agreed I might take the coach home and skip the wedding itself — even they weren't heartless enough to force me to suffer through that.

I was also in the cellar on the day after the wedding when the odd gift appeared at the manse. Mother retrieved me to the salon where she'd directed the package put, then she and father left me alone with the large package. I tore off the fabric wrapping to find a large, embellished silver-edged mirror and a card signed, *My apologies, Werner.* He must have sent it before the wedding, and my anger at him, at our situation, at the loss of my love welled up hot and fast. I was preparing to smash it to pieces on the stone hearth when Grandmother entered the salon.

"Stop! Adalee! What are you doing?"

I whirled around, ready to unleash my frustrations on the bent-over woman standing by the hearth. Under her sickly skin and thin, white hair, I could see the beautiful woman she must have been when she was younger. *Poor Grandmother,* I thought as I held the mirror aloft. My heart quivered, my fury waning a bit.

"You lied, Grandmother! You said the potion would take time to work, but it hasn't worked!"

Grandmother clasped her hands in front of her chest and chuckled at me.

"Oh, but it has. Look at you! Your ability with spells is better than mine. And when was the last time you thought on Werner until yesterday? So what if I gave you a potion that made you better at spells? It had the same effect, did it not?"

I stilled, lowering the mirror which was growing heavy in my arms. So she hadn't given me a heartache potion? Oh, Grandmother was a still river that ran so very, very deep — deep enough to drown in.

And as much as I despised admitting it, she was right. Spells and potions blossomed with ease under my fingertips. I read her ancient book as well as any book in my father's library. And until I attended Werner's' wedding pageant, I hadn't thought on the prince at all.

She held out a herb-stained hand to me. "Come. Bring your cloak and that mirror. We might as well put it to good use."

The decrepit stairs darkened as we descended, and Grandmother lit more torches in the cellar, bathing the shadowy space in flickering light. I placed the mirror against the wall where Grandmother directed and stepped back, wrapping my cloak around my body, trying to hide from the vile thing. What was she going to do with this cursed mirror?

"It's not cursed," she said, reading my thoughts. "Werner may have to wed another, but that doesn't mean his heart lies with her. This mirror is his way of reminding you that you are beautiful, that he thinks you are the most beautiful woman he's ever met. But a mirror can show you more than your skin. A good mirror can show you your true heart."

I stared at my reflection, dappled and wavering in the torchlight, and I studied myself. I dropped my hood so my rich chestnut hair fell in lush waves on my shoulders. I hadn't brushed it in days, yet it still shone in the incandescent light. The black velvet of my cloak set off my milky skin, making it look like fine porcelain. Not even a freckle marred my skin. The cellar shadows highlighted the sharp edge of my jaw and cheekbones. And my gray eyes sparkled in a silvery glow, possessive and commanding. All that I easily saw in the mirror.

But what was this true heart my grandmother spoke of?

The woman herself puttered around behind me, gathering her necessaries and standing on tiptoes to reach a black book set high on a shelf and covered in cobwebs. I reached easily over her head and grabbed if off the shelf.

"Thank you, sweet. Come over here. We are going to transform this mirror from what you think is cursed to something charmed. We will make it a magic mirror, and with all your newfound talents, you will be able to make this mirror work to your advantage."

She flipped through the old book without a care for its shriveled, crumbling pages, until she found the spell she wanted.

This book didn't have the shimmery lettering as the other book, and appeared untouched for years, decades even. Whatever this book was, she didn't use it as much as her other book. Maybe for good reason.

"Grandmother, are you sure about this?" I asked as I studied her confident movements. She claimed I was talented, but I knew I would never move with her assurance. And with a rarely used book? Suddenly, none of this seemed like a good idea. I wasn't a witch, good or no, after all.

She nodded. "Give me your hand. Since it's *your* mirror, you'll need to put the recipe together."

Lifting my hand, she turned it over and sprinkled grounds into my palm then dumped them into her small cauldron on the table – bigger than her usual bowl and able to hold all the contents. After doing that with several grounds, she dropped my hand and handed me a smelly liquid to add to the mix.

"Vitriol," she answered my unspoken question as I poured in several explosive drops.

Once it was all mixed to her satisfaction, she handed me a rag that had seen better days and pointed to the cauldron.

"Dip the rag and wipe it on the mirror. Cover every inch of the mirror, not a single crevice or curve can be missed. Wipe every crease, every cranny. Wipe it over and over. I'll leave you to it."

Then she waddled out and left me. I stood there stupidly, an old rag hanging from my fingers, trying to figure out what just happened. Sighing inwardly, I did as she directed and dipped the rag in the stinky, oily tincture and began to wipe the mirror.

As I worked, I grew oddly focused on the mirror, on the work of polishing it. Soon there was nothing in that dim cellar but myself and this mirror that glowed under my hands. The more I rubbed, the more the mirror glowed, until it seemed to have a life of its own.

The reflective surface shimmered at the center, and I paused to toss the rag onto the table. As I had before, I stared at my reflection which was now somehow different, like a whisper-thin caul covered me. Grandmother had claimed the mirror could show my true heart. Was it ready to do that now?

"Oh, Mirror," I said under my breath, "what is it you're supposed to show me?"

I expected nothing. Grandmother might have made potions and spells for years, but to charm a mirror? That was something altogether different. Strange, even.

Yet, as I stared at the mirror, the center of it swirled, lightly at first, then in a smoky thickness that obscured my reflection. From that foggy center, another face appeared. A face but not a face. A translucent figure of closed eyes, cheeks, nose and mouth — definitely not *my* reflection. I glanced around the cellar, trying to discern if this were nothing more than a trick of the flickering candlelight.

"Magic Mirror?" I whispered.

I reached out a tentative finger to touch the smooth glass, only to find it somehow less firm, more malleable than a mirror ought to be.

The eyes flipped open, and I jumped back, gathering my cloak around my chest like a shield.

"Yes, my queen?" the mirror asked, its voice deep and resonating in the depths of the cellar. I shivered under my cape.

Queen? What type of mirror is this?

"What are you?" I asked, leaning forward only a smidgen. Curious though I was about this mysterious glass, my mother didn't raise a fool.

"I am your Magic Mirror. You can ask me anything, and I will answer with the full truth as I see it. I am a mirror into the depths of yourself."

At this, my lips twisted and I raised an eyebrow. An enigmatic mirror, more like it. I decided to test this supposed magic mirror.

"Magic Mirror, who's the fairest in all this land?"

The smoke behind the faint face swirled. "With eyes of silver and skin without flaw, you, my queen, are the fairest of them all."

My lips twisted all the more. Of course, the mirror would respond with a compliment, and I chided myself for asking such a childish question. Time to try something harder.

"Why did Werner give me this mirror?"

More swirling smoke. "Though a new lady holds his title to start, you alone yet hold his heart."

As much as I didn't want it to happen, my heart fluttered under my breast. Would the mirror always speak in mystery?

"To start? What does that mean?"

"Her time is limited, and in years, the title to you will be fitted."

At this, I stumbled away from the mirror. That was something I had not considered — that Berta might expire before her time and leave Werner alone. And ready to wed another. Ready to wed me.

Grandmother had said she didn't know of something that could tell her the future. Was it because she'd never had a mirror like this? Why had she not cast this spell before? Could this mirror really foretell the future?

My mind whirled like the smoke in the mirror. That was why the mirror called me queen —

I'd step into the role soon enough. I dared not ask how soon. Instead, I threw the cloth back over the mirror, whispered a quick thank you, and raced for the stairs.

If I were to wed Werner one day, I needed to make sure I appeared as young as I do now. I made a mental note to ask Grandmother about youthful potions. I wanted to make sure I seemed as though no time, not a day, had passed between us. Nothing would change, and when the day arrived, we'd love each the same as we do now.

Werner might not know the true value of the gift he'd sent me, but this mirror would hang close at hand for the rest of my days. Stopping at the first step, I turned and rushed back to the mirror. I grasped it in grateful, protective hands and carried it up to my room.

I had many, many more questions for this mirror.

Chapter Four

A FEW NIGHTS later, before the servants presented supper, I knocked on Grandmother's door. My body fairly buzzed — I wanted to tell her how wonderfully the mirror had worked, how excited I was at the news the mirror shared — but no answer.

She'd been busy in her cottage and Mother had kept me busy at the manse with the most mundane tasks. But then, what tasks didn't seem mundane to me now that I had the light of magic at my fingertips?

New dresses, sewing, cleaning my chambers, even a ride into town. My mother's bright eyes rejoiced that I'd joined her, and she pretended not to notice my sulking. I craved returning to my mirror and Grandmother's cellar. The first moment I had to myself, I scrambled across the grassy courtyard to the ramshackle cottage.

"Grandmother!" I pounded harder, shaking the warped door in its frame, yet nothing.

Perchance she was asleep. In her advanced age, she'd taken to napping before the evening meal, and today had been a busy day. I knocked harder.

"Grandmother?" I called to the cream-colored door. "Grandmother!"

My patience was at an end. With no answer, I cracked the door open slightly, so the fading light of day poured in a brilliant shaft of light into her room. I barely made out her shape on her four-poster bed tucked into the corner of her house.

"Grandmother?" I called out in a lighter tone. I didn't want to scare her awake. "Grandmother, supper is near ready. And I wanted to tell you about that mirror. It worked perfectly. Grandmother?"

My hearted pounded in my chest, and the buzzing under my skin became a nervous shake. Why wasn't she waking?

"Grandmother?"

I threw the door open and lifted my skirts to run to her bed. She should be waking up. She should be answering my questions and sharing in my excitement. I laid my hands on her shoulder and head, and I immediately knew. Her skin was papery and cool — too cool. And she still didn't move.

My beloved grandmother had passed on her skills, her secret cellar, and gifted me a shockingly talented mirror. Her work on this earth was done, and while she was napping, she passed into the great beyond.

I laid on the bed next to her, curling my body around her lifeless back, and held her as I cried. I sobbed my heart out — my grandmother had been my heart since I'd been a wee girl in stained dresses and dirty feet. She'd been my foundation, my greatest supporter, and with the knowledge of spells and her cellar, she'd given me the most astounding gift.

And now she was gone.

How was I going to survive without her? Who would teach me now?

I survived by throwing myself into the mysteries of her cellar. Losing Werner followed by Grandmother was enough to cause any woman to lose her senses, but Grandmother's cellar, now my cellar, saved me.

We buried Grandmother on a late summer day, before the leaves started to change. A large willow tree shaded her grave site, its leaves and branches bowing under the same sorrow that crushed my chest. Mother and Father wanted me to throw dirt onto her grave, but I couldn't do it. I glared at my parents, whose less-than-sage advice was for me to "not think about it." In those moments, I hated my parents. How could I not think about the woman who'd changed the course of my life?

Instead, I escaped to my magic cellar. I spent hours, days, months, pouring over books, practicing the spells, mixing the herbs and potions. My skin paled even more, making my silvery-gray eyes stand out in stark contrast, my chestnut hair look more rich. Mother complained at dinner nearly every night, chiding me for hiding away in the cellar. Only when I promised her that I was just studying and painting did she quiet her tongue.

I exuded scents of lilac and summer grass and bergamot as I practiced with youth potions, and I had to lie again to Mother, tell her I was experimenting with perfumes — a hobby she adored. Periodically, I gifted her a small jar of flowery water. It bought me more time with my herbs and potions.

I grew almost exotic in my appearance, one I hoped Werner would love when we reunited.

My mirror also became my escape. It hung in my chambers, next to my vanity, and I spoke to it every day. The mirror became my sanctuary, and the more I spoke to it, the more I relied on its words. I felt assured, more confident with every passing day. I woke each morning, anxious to see that swirling surface and live my life based on its responses.

And though I hated to admit it, my first question every day was the same — "Who's the fairest of them all?" I should have felt some manner of shame at my vanity, but I didn't.

I had to know. I had to make sure that when Werner was ready to wed me again, I looked beautiful. Every morning, the mirror assured me I was.

Then I learned Queen Berta was pregnant. *Pregnant*.

That I hadn't expected — a punch to the stomach that consumed me. I clutched at the neckline of my gown and cried and cried. That was supposed to be *my* baby, with *my* husband!

The mirror hadn't shared that information about Berta being with child, and a violent urge rose from my aching belly to smash it with a rock. I'd even grabbed one from the garden and was holding it aloft when Grandmother's voice spoke in my head, reminding me of the magical import of the mirror.

All my vigor fled from my body, and I sagged against the fool filigree frame. Instead, I took to my bed for weeks with the curtains closed, and I didn't emerge until I managed to temper my emotions. The mirror helped — it continually told me that Werner and I were still destined to be one, child or no.

But I was starting to disbelieve it. A little. Magic or not.

They had a girl, and I found some comfort in that. *I* would have given him his son. Yet, the babe was rumored to be the most beautiful baby in all of Switzerland, with Werner's coal-black hair and her mother's tender features and bright blue eyes. She was merely a babe, yet my question to my mirror grew more urgent every day.

Over and over, the mirror proclaimed my beauty above all.

Chapter Five

ONE DAY, MONTHS after my life had been upended so bitterly and abruptly, I attended the market with Emma. She strolled ahead of me, selecting wares to refill the pantry for the fall. Our manse had gardens and orchards that stocked the pantry well, but some items, particularly dried fish and my father's favorite sausages, could only be found at the market. Mother had also given Emma a list of necessities: French lavender soap, ribbons, white refined sugar.

The sugar was telling, and I grinned to myself whenever I thought on it. I had tried a few different health potions on my father, with Grandmother's help and without. I couldn't be sure which one had the outcome I'd desired, but my father had soon stopped taking his beloved cakes after supper. And he only had one biscuit during tea instead of his regular four. Healthy pink had started to return to his pasty cheeks. If his belly were shirking, I couldn't tell from dress shirts and surcoats, but mother's face stopped tightening at every meal, and that told me more than anything else. Evidently, in the privacy of their quarters, she noted the weight loss.

So white sugar had started to come back into the house. Not often, but present nonetheless.

I had tried a few other potions and spells, but only in the sanctuary of my cellar until one of the house maids asked for my help in finding the locket heirloom she'd lost. Finding item spells were simple, too easy. After swearing the maid to secrecy under the threat of losing her position in our house, I burned peppermint and had her visualize the item in her hand whilst she chanted a phrase from Grandmother's book. She found it later that day. I told her the same thing Grandmother had told me, that we were just putting her desires into the universe. The maid seemed to buy it. Of course she would, as ecstatic as she was to find the locket.

It was a chancy thing to do — Grandmother would be horrified that I let anyone else know I was practicing magic, but the maid had been so distraught, it tore at my heart. Maybe there was something to be said for sharing a skill when it was needed. Hiding my magic, or not using it when needed, seemed selfish.

If the other spells worked, I had no confirmation. A child's dog may have found its own way home without my help. A sore may have healed on its own without my chanting the words. I can't prove that my potion, my spell, commanded those things to happen.

But I liked to believe I had a hand in the matter.

And seeing my father slowly come back to stronger health only made me more secure in my abilities. They had been slow to bloom, but as Grandmother had promised, they were blooming. The more I worked with them, the better I'd become. Magic was coming to me rather easily, as of late.

I'd lied to Emma, telling her I wanted to shop for a gift for my parents. She bought the excuse readily enough. After all the work she did daily for our family, I was sure she enjoyed a bit of market time to herself. If I loitered at the market, the longer she might dally.

The first stall I sought out was the apothecary. I'd ordered from him before, requesting basic herbs sent to the manse, but today was the first time I'd been able to shop and perchance find items that might have raised my mother's eyebrows if they were included in a delivery.

Certain items I didn't even need to purchase. Crushed eggshells, bergamot, and spiders' legs were freely available at home. Crushed crab shells? Sulfur powder? Blue Moon water? Those selections needed to be purchased with a bit more care. And my stores, formerly Grandmother's stores, were low. I really needed to stock up.

Monsieur Johan Muller, the apothecary and a handsome older man with silver streaks glistening in his black hair and intense hazel eyes that made even the most staunch man squirm, perched on a stool behind his counter, his sleeves rolled up as he worked his pestle. I waited for him to pause, and when he turned to me, I gave him the widest smile possible.

"Monsieur Muller," I greeted him. His expression didn't change, not even a twitch of his lips. "I have an extensive list of scripts that I must fill. Can you provide these to me?"

His strong hand snatched the list from me, and he slipped a monocle over one eye as he studied the list.

"Everything but the Blue Moon water. I broke my last bottle. You'll have to wait until I can go to Zurich to obtain more."

"Merde," I cursed under her breath.

Grandmother had none left, at least none that I had found, and several of her potions called for it. I'd have to raid her books to see if I might find the recipe to make it on my own.

Johan eyed me from under drooped lids as he set my herbals into my linen sack. "Odd ingredients for a well-to-do daughter of a baron," he commented. "Are you doing something more with them?"

I threw my head back to glare at him directly. Obviously, I wasn't going to tell him what my grandmother had taught me — witches weren't popular, only necessary — and I didn't want any word of my work in the cellar getting back to my parents. Mother would have a fit if she learned I spent my days in a dingy, cob-webbed cellar creating potions. Grandmother had managed to keep it a secret, and I vowed not to betray her legacy.

I traced a slender, white finger along the length of his table. "You never know when an ingredient might be useful," I answered him enigmatically, but my voice was innocent enough.

He shrugged and continued to measure out and pack the items. "In the future, I can have items delivered to you personally. With soaps or hair oil on top, and the ingredients packed in straw underneath, hidden from the casual eye."

Ahh, so he wasn't trying to out me, rather retain me as a customer. And truly, the wealthy baron's daughter was a fine paying client indeed. He never had to worry about a billet not being paid. Pursing my lips into a knowing smile, I gave him a curt nod.

"Well, then, here are your herbals." He handed the sack over the counter, and I held out several francs to him, which he eagerly plucked from my grasp. Yes, he wanted me as a customer indeed. I gave him another nod in goodbye, certain my secret would be safe with him.

Now I needed to find a gift for my parents to keep my secret from the rest of my household.

Only my secret wasn't as well-kept as I'd believed. Either the maid did say something to someone else, or my interest in the apothecary caught the attention of someone in the market. It didn't matter. All that did matter was someone tugging on my cape. I swiveled in the patchy grass to find a petite blonde woman standing behind me.

She shrunk back from me when I turned, but she didn't run away. She wanted something from me. I narrowed my eyes at her.

"Is there something you want?" I asked. My tone was a bit too harsh, and what little color the woman held on her skin vanished. Only then did I note the bruise on her face, a stark purple against her pale skin. I paused and leaned down to her.

She was shorter than I by almost a head, a pretty little thing with a ragged kirtle, light amber eyes, and hair like sunset. But what I noticed most about her was how she seemed to cower under my gaze.

Something was wrong with this poor woman. Why was she reaching out to me? Did she think my father and his connections might help her? We gave plenty in charity every month — donations and alms had their own entry in Father's ledger — and she could beg at the house if she needed money. Father often chastised Mother for her overly-generous nature. If this woman wanted a position at the Baron's house, in that she'd be unsuccessful. Mother wasn't hiring any maids presently.

"You, you are the one who can help someone when no one else can?"

Her question was little more than a breath on the wind. I stiffened at her odd question.

"I fear I don't know what you are asking. I don't help anyone. My father, the Baron, might —"

She shook her head fiercely, her light hair falling into her face. "No, not the good Baron." She leaned into me as her eyes shifted back and forth around the market. "Yourself. That you have a touch."

Her last word was so low a whisper I had to strain to hear it. A touch?

I leaned back. I knew what she meant. Beads of sweat formed on my back and rolled down my spine. How had she found out?

The maid. She must have told someone. No wonder Grandmother kept her skills so dark a secret. No one ever outed her.

"What did she tell you?" I asked in a hard tone. What would happen to me, my parents, our household if it was discovered that I dabbled in magic? I might be burned as a witch. Mobs didn't care if it was white or black magic when it came to burning at the stake.

"Nothing. No one told me anything. But some rumors from your house about your father's increasing health and how things don't remain lost in your manse have reached my ears. I have no other options. I beg of you to help me."

I mimicked the young woman and glanced around the market. People milled about and few paid any attention to us. Yet, I'd rather not have anyone overhear this woman's words, so I took her hand and dragged her around the side of the governor's building. This side, opposite the market, was shaded and empty. Not even grass grew here.

"Tell me. Tell me what you know. What do you want?"

I stumbled backward when the woman fell to her knees and wrapped her arms around my legs.

"My mother died several years ago, and I've been raising my younger siblings. My father, he takes too much drink and can be violent. But we need him. His money supports us, but I can't let him —"

She stopped her outpouring of words as they turned to sobbing. A hard lump formed in my throat as I sagged against the wall. Then I reached for her hands to help her rise.

"Come, stand up and tell me what you want."

"My father's not a bad man, just a drinker with a bad temper. He's always had a heavy hand with me, but I can handle it. Lately, though, he's taken to laying his fists on my younger brother and sister. Surely you can help us."

I licked my lips. I understood what she was asking. My mind flicked to Grandmother's cellar and the collection of books. I'd never had to use any such potion, but I was sure those precious books held a solution to this girl's problem. I only feared it might come from the lesser-used book on the high shelf. While I shook my head, I found myself saying yes against my better judgment. How could I deny her wretched request?

"Come to my house later today, but not the front door. Come around to the small house at the back of the Baron's property. Knock and I'll receive you there."

I wouldn't bring her to the beloved secret cellar, but Grandmother's house stood empty, and I could meet her there. She nodded eagerly. I wracked my brain. What might I possibly need to help her? What might the potions call for? I tapped at my chin with a fingernail as I pondered.

"Bring with you a snippet of your father's hair and a piece of fabric from his clothing," I told her. "That should be all I need from you."

The girl nodded vigorously again. I had to suppress the desire to reach out and pat her like a puppy. What had this girl and her family gone through to make her so desperate? An odd sensation filled me, one that wasn't borne of kindness or pity, but one of anger and justice.

"What's your name?" I asked.

The girl bowed her head. "Isabelle," she answered quietly.

I patted her again. "Well, Isabelle, we will see what we can do to solve your problem. Meet me where I told you right before sundown."

Isabelle's eyes watered and she grabbed my hand, kissing it. Then she dropped my hand, lifted her frayed skirts, and raced back to the market.

Isabelle's knock was like a bird's wing upon the door, soft and hesitant. I'd had the good sense to remove my black cape before the young woman arrived, lest I frightened her with my witch-like appearance. I loved the cape, but it tended to make me look dark and brooding. And the poor girl seemed frightened enough as it was.

She rushed into the cottage and sat on the stool at the table I pointed to. My required implements were prepared, including the leather-bound book open to the proper spell, ready for use. Finding the right potion, *that* had been quite a problem.

Who would have thought Grandmother didn't have a specific potion for stopping someone from violence? So many were designed to solve other concerns which might lead them to lesser violence — a potion to dispel anger, a spell to quell mob fear — but for a man who raised his fists to his family? Nothing specifically for that.

As I reviewed the white magic recipe I intended to use, Isabelle opened her tight fist to drop a lock of hair and a crumpled swatch of wool onto the table.

The spell I did find and decide on seemed perfect. Grandmother, or whoever wrote the recipe, had titled it with an air of humor *Calming Lyssa*, after the Greek spirit of anger. Over time, the more I perused Grandmother's books, the more I giggled at the oddly comical titles. A bit of levity amid dire work, perhaps?

From the expression on Isabelle's face, now was not the time for joviality, so I kept the name of the potion to myself. I set to work on her white magic spell. Once the potion was ready, I steeped it into a tea-like drink and sealed it in a jar, then handed it to the dazzled Isabelle.

"Add this to his drink of choice. You should notice a different a day or two."

She gave the drink a sour look, peering at it through the jar. "That's it? Are you sure it will work?"

My mind went to my grandmother's claims, as I'd experienced the same qualm when I'd lost Werner, then again with regards to my father's weight. I gave Isabelle a tight smile.

"No, I can't guarantee the potion will work. But we must begin by putting it out into the heavens first. Then we shall see what happens."

I had confidence it would work — most of Grandmother's spells from her book worked like, well, like magic.

Isabelle cupped the jar in both hands, almost as if she feared she'd drop it or lose it on her way home. Then she paused, dipping her gaze to the precocious jar in her hands.

"I don't have any —" she tried to say, and I knew what worried her.

"I won't take any value for the potion until we know it works. Then we can discuss any sort of payment."

Relief overwhelmed Isabelle, softening her face and relaxing the stiffness in her shoulders. She nodded once, then departed quickly, most eager to be gone from the Baron's lands and the mysterious cottage.

Whether it was to hurry to use the potion or because she feared me, I didn't know.

At least, not yet.

Before the Magic Mirror

Chapter Six

SHOCK WAS TOO fine a word to express how I felt when I saw Isabelle storming up to me in my mother's gardens. I quickly searched the bushes and trees, making sure no one saw the girl approach, then raced to the edge of the property to meet her.

Once I was close enough, I readily saw the reason for her return. The discoloration on her face from the day before was now a solid black and purple bruise. I halted my steps, my hand covering my mouth. What had happened?

"Isabelle!" I called out. "What happened? Didn't you use the potion?"

She threw the jar at me. She missed, but the jar landed hard on the ground where it smashed into pieces. It was empty — only a few drops of remaining potion stained the dirt. I spun to look at her again and gasped as she rushed me, her face brilliantly red with fury.

"You lied! You said if he drank it, he'd stop drinking, and that he'd not be violent with us! The potion made him angrier! And he took it out on me and my brothers!"

Isabelle's pasty white hands gripped her skirts as she railed at me. When she paused for a breath, I squatted and retrieved the broken glass, lest someone cut themselves on it as they walked in the garden. I turned the pieces over in my hands, perplexed.

Why hadn't it worked?

Every other potion and spell I'd concocted with Grandmother had been successful. Even helping the maid find her locket, and that was after Grandmother's passing. What had happened this time? Could I only do magic while she was alive? Then why had the maid's spell worked?

What had I done wrong?

Or, what if Grandmother's presumption of putting the desire out to the universe wasn't accurate? What if Grandmother had been wrong? That white spells and potions were somehow limited in what they might do?

I was so consumed with these thoughts, trying to figure out what had failed in the potion, that I hadn't heard the woman speak.

"Adalee!" she screeched at me, and I swiveled and rose to face her. "You said it would work! Now we must do something else, otherwise he will kill one of us for sure!"

This time, I recoiled, thinking she was surely going to strike me. And though a shaft of fear struck down my spine, I also understood her anger — what impotent fury had thrust through me when Werner had left and I dreaded life without him? That dread no longer fastened its crippling grip on me, and something inside my chest bloomed like a bloody flower in a dark forest. A new, strange desire to rise to this challenge, to know that *I* controlled my magic — it didn't control me.

I didn't care if I had to use the black magic books. I'd help this young woman find her relief. Not for her, truly. Her father's condition was her problem, not mine. But that fact the potion had failed — that was my problem. I couldn't abide by that.

I needed to prove to myself that I could use my magic at *my* will.

"Isabelle, come with me. I had hoped a lighter potion would work, but it appears we need something stronger, more potent, for your father. But it might have some adverse effects as a result. The harder the magic, the more of a toll it takes, and the cost can be dear." I tried to be clear with her, yet her fury closed her ears to anything I might say to convince her otherwise.

"I don't care!" Isabelle screamed wildly, her voice rising. "Whatever the effect is, it can't be as bad as my father!"

I chewed at the inside of my lip. She was desperate, oh so desperate. And people who were desperate don't think as clearly as they should. I knew from experience. The decision, however, was already made.

I risked resting a cool hand on her arm. "Fine. Come with me to my cottage. I'll have to search my books for the proper recipe. Do you have time?"

From the look of her, she wasn't going back to her father's house any time soon, at least not until she had a potion or spell from me. She nodded once, abruptly. I turned toward the cottage, and she followed.

I grabbed the older, crumbling-cover book from a high shelf, a book Grandmother had shown me but never used in my presence. The thin onion skin paper threatened to disintegrate under my touch. With a delicate finger, I perused the list of recipes while Isabelle sat patiently on her stool. Well, as patiently as she could muster — she only fidgeted a little bit.

The book was heavy with magic. When I touched the pages, a vibration started in my fingertips and twisted and curved up my arm to my head and chest, a powerful, thrilling sensation. No wonder Grandmother had cautioned me about this magic!

A few recipes might have worked — a protection spell, for example. But those tended to wear off, and what if I couldn't protect her brothers, too? Only Isabelle was here with me. An empowerment potion? I flicked my gaze briefly to Isabelle, then back at my book. Her papery skin and bony body screamed a need for empowerment, but I didn't think it would work the way she wanted. She'd still have to stand up to her father with that potion. A banishing spell? No, she'd said she needed her father in the house for finances and support. Banishing wouldn't do Isabelle or her brothers any good.

My finger caressed the page down to one that stood out above all the rest. Yes, *this* was the one she needed. A spell to prevent mistreatment. Perfect.

But it was a dark spell, a spell designed to modify a person dramatically from the inside out. Not a tiny, light spell to eat a bit less or find a misplaced locket. No, this was a spell that changed a person's behavior. Changed who they *were*.

It was also my first dark spell. Grandmother had told me how high the cost might be, but for this, for children who were already paying so dear a price? I shrugged it off. The cost couldn't be that high.

And from the looks of this poor, desperate girl, any cost was worth it.

The words seemed to dance on the page as I read them and began to collect the necessary items.

She'd brought fabric and a snippet of his hair again — desperate, but a clever girl. This time, once I had mixed all the ingredients (several of which that caused Isabelle to wrinkle her nose), I lifted my arm, long under my draping cape, and said the archaic words aloud.

Only, they sounded more like a curse to my ears, and they must have to Isabelle's too, for she shrunk away from me as I called them out.

Did the room of Grandmother's cottage suddenly darken? Did the wind pick up outside as I chanted? Maybe it was my imagination.

Then, instead of putting the liquid potion in a jar, I lit it all on fire. A burst of green flame shot up, knocking me backwards and Isabelle off her stool. Fear crossed her features, followed by something else. Her eyes narrowed slightly. Yes, if I didn't miss my mark, the look on her face was expectation.

This potion, this *spell*, for it could truly be called nothing else, was destined to work.

She departed quickly, the packet of ashes from the potion tucked in her waistband. I'd instructed her to put it in his food, that he must eat it directly. And unlike white spells, dark ones worked rather quickly. Then I wished her good luck and shoved her out the door.

I locked the ancient lock and turned to lean my back against the rough-hewn oak wood door. The breath I exhaled, long and wavering, released my shaking nerves along with it. I'd hidden my shaking hands and nervous voice from Isabelle. Now that she was gone, every concern I'd had about my first black spell rose in my head in a pounding headache.

What if it didn't work? What if the cost was too dear? What if I messed it up and the cost happened with no effect? So many questions, so many chances to get it wrong.

No, I told myself, rubbing my hands together under the sweeping sleeves of my cloak. *No, it had to work.* I'd done everything the book commanded. The spell *would* work.

And it must have, because I didn't see Isabelle at all the next day. Nor the day after that. After the third day, a sense of peace settled over me. It must have been successful, and my thoughts turned from Isabelle and her potion to other household concerns.

It wasn't until a fortnight later that I received any verification about the cursed spell. Isabelle found me in the market — crept up to me more like it. The air was cool — fall had claimed her treasure and marked it for all to see in hues of golds and auburns, but not cold. With so temperate a day, I let my hood fall down and my rich tresses pool around my shoulders. The breeze lifted small tendrils that tickled my cheeks, and my chest vibrated with excitement at the changing seasons.

Isabelle, though, wore a cape, too. Not as luxuriant as mine, threadbare even, but the hood was wide and up, covering her hair and face almost completely. When I turned away from the smithy's stall, she grabbed at my cape again, only I didn't recognize her right away.

"Isabelle! I didn't see you there, hiding in your cape!" I gave her a weak smile and waved her over to the grassy area at the end of the stalls. "So, did it work?"

I kept my voice low, conspiratorial. My heart hammered in my chest, echoing the smithy. Had my first time dabbling in black magic worked?

Isabelle's tight smile was unreadable. She nodded briefly, and my heart thumped out of my chest and soared.

I did it! I had made the magic my own!

Then Isabelle's smile shifted, appearing almost sad as the edges of her lips drooped. I froze where I stood. *What had the magic done?*

"What is it, Isabelle?"

Wordlessly, she shifted the hood so the right side of her face caught the pale sunlight, and my gasp escaped before I could slam my hand over my mouth.

Whatever the price was, the cost for the spell, could I say it was worth this? No, only Isabelle could be the judge, and no wonder she wasn't talking. When she finally did, only the left side of her mouth moved with ease.

"I don't blame you," she said in a terse voice, her lips moving slightly, uncomfortably. "I asked for the potion, demanded it from you, and you warned me of the cost. I just hadn't known the cost would be like this, especially since my bruises hadn't even healed when my skin burned."

Burned? A vitriol burn, an oil burn maybe, from the puckering. Had some splashed on her face as she changed scones or filled a lamp? The skin gathered and puckered from her cheekbone to her lips. She was scarred for life.

"The worst is my younger brother. His clothing caught fire. He yet lives, so we are blessed, but his skin will never be the same. He will never be the same. The doctors claim it was a miracle he didn't die. But you and I know the truth. There was a cost to be paid, wasn't there?"

Isabelle's eyes were still as bright as ever, intense with her suggestion, and I nodded under her staunch gaze.

"Does your father —?" I tried to ask, but I couldn't form the words. What if all this pain had been for naught?

Isabelle nodded. "I must give you credit where it is due. He's not laid a hand on any of us since. He's not taken to drink, nor stolen money. He appears happier, and our household, barring the burns, is a happier place."

I tried to find a sense of joy in her words but failed. She gave me another one of those chest-clenching smiles and leaned into me. I called on every ounce of will power not to shrink away from her.

"*Oui*, Adalee, the spell worked just as you said. But that magic, it's a dangerous magic. Think on it hard before you use it again."

Then Isabelle replaced her hood, lifted the hem of her cape so it didn't drag in the dirt, and marched away. Her life changed — both for the better, and for the worse.

To be scarred so terribly — was it worth it for her to have a loving father? I stared at Isabelle as she walked away. Only she could answer that question.

Would I have accepted so harsh a fate if our roles were reversed? For that, I had no answer. I had nightmares of her hideously scarred skin for weeks after market day.

Before the Magic Mirror

Chapter Seven

WERNER NEVER RETURNED for me, and I doubted my mirror's premonition on it. Months, seasons, years dragged on, and still no Werner. Perhaps my mirror wasn't so magic after all.

After a few years, I pushed thought of Werner to the back of my mind and let my potion and spell interests take over. My life passed like this for time — keeping to myself, my cellar, and only working with positive white spells and potions, giving small, mild recipes a try and helping those when they did ask for small things, like love tokens or finding potions.

Though I longed to try more of the black spells, to practice and refine them and make then work, my experience with Isabelle remained too sore a reminder. And I was glad my mirror hadn't been in the room where I'd crafted the darker spell. It already cautioned and chastised me for dallying where I shouldn't. I didn't want to hear its lecturing again. So I kept those spells hidden away, determined to follow Grandmother's guidance, and too afraid to see what cost those spells might incur. I'd only started sleeping through the night again as we neared Christmas.

Plus, I had no need for the dark magic. I may not have been happy, but I was content with my life.

My parents, aging as they were, however, weren't content, and they had sought out other suitors, handsome, landed men of noble houses to vie for my hand. I cringed inwardly every time I thought of those eager men and my desperate parents.

Yet none of them were Werner — how could I marry one of them when my mirror vowed that Werner and I would be reunited one day? Though the mirror might be wrong, I clung onto what little hope it provided.

The last man my parents had brought to the house had been a joke. To marry him would have brought shame on my father's good name. Why had they even considered the man?

More than ten years passed since Werner and his father had broken the marriage contract — perchance that was the kindling to my parents burning desire to see me wed. I well know that it was a difficult thing to find a husband for an aged woman such as I, but I didn't need a husband. Werner would be marrying me one day; I didn't want help finding a husband.

But I couldn't exactly share that secret with my parents. They had no knowledge of my secret cellar, my magic practice, or my mirror that promised a future with Werner was assured. Instead, I had to suffer one pathetic suitor after another.

"Adalee," my mother's shrill voice drifted up the stairs, grating on every last nerve. *Ugh*, another suitor made his appearance. "Come down and meet Baron Von Scuffer's son. He has traveled quite the distance just to meet you."

I grimaced at my reflection in the mirror. I patted my hair, which Emma had twisted into an intricate coiffure with embedded jewels and gold chain, and brushed at my light, moss-colored gown with puffed sleeves and ribbon that fell to elbows. Even as supposedly aged as I was, the image in the mirror reflected a stunningly beautiful woman. I sighed as I stretched my white kid gloves onto my arms, grateful for the practice of gloves in social settings so I wouldn't have to touch the cretin. I was the picture of the perfect lady.

"Adalee!" my mother called again. I huffed in response — it wasn't fair to pre-judge the man before I met him. Yet, after the previous suitors, I didn't have high expectations.

"Coming, mother!" I responded down the steps and rose from the vanity. Time to set this poor man on his way.

I lifted the hem of my filmy gown as I descended the steps. The man standing at the bottom was nothing like I'd expected, and I paused on the stairwell, trying to take him in.

His soft brown eyes gazed up at me, full of awe and hope, and his light brown hair sat in shiny waves to his collar. He cut a fit figure in his brown velvet waistcoat, and despite myself, my heart went out to him. He was everything puppy dogs and sunrises and gentle waves on the river.

"Adalee, I'd like to introduce Simon Von Scuffer."

My mother had also taken the time to dress for the occasion, her blue brocade bright in the sunlight pouring through the salon windows. I nodded at her and collected myself, then finished my slow walk down the steps. Simon grasped my gloved fingers in a light touch and kissed the fabric at the back of my hand.

"*Enchantée*," he said in a low, husky voice. Oh, if my heart weren't already committed, I could easily lose it to him. Even his voice was as velvet as the rest of him.

"Why don't you go sit in the garden and make acquaintances before supper?" my mother offered with a wide smile.

My own smile broke a little at her expression — I hadn't seen my mother this happy in years.

"I would love that," Simon answered and extended his elbow. I threaded my hand though his arm and let him escort me outside.

Autumn hadn't fully enveloped the land, so the leaves changed while the warm air lingered. The gardens were in the twilight of their bloom — a few peony and rose bushes painted their colors among the winding pathways, punctuated with a marble statue that my mother received as a Christmas gift from my father several years before and the stone bench upon which Simon and I sat. A light breeze lifted my hair and bathed us in those heady, early autumn scents.

I had thought this moment might be awkward, as Simon's romantic attempts fell on a hard shell. My heart was dedicated elsewhere.

But it wasn't. Simon gave me a bit of space and engaged me in light conversation — about my childhood, my family, about his own passion for horses.

"Do you have stables? I would love to see them," he said, and I was taken aback.

My other suitors had feigned interest in me, comparing me to the blooms that surrounded us, or spent most of their time speaking with my parents. A genuine sharing of interests? Maybe Simon had more to him than I gave him credit for.

"Yes, at the rear of the manse. Not as large as yours, of course, but we have two Franches-Montagnes and a Clydesdale."

Simon's brown eyes, so like a doe I'd seen exploring the garden once, widened. "I would love to see them."

He held my arm formally, not overstepping, and once again, I marveled at him and his under-bearing ways. I led him along one of the florid trails to the stables. Archie, the stable hand, waved at us and moved out of way so we could move easily to the stalls.

Simon appeared most interested in the giant Clydesdale, not that I blamed him. The animal that my father affectionately called Zeus was a gentle giant, and he nuzzled Simon's hand as I introduced them. Most likely Zeus was searching for an apple or carrot in Simon's palm, but he loved the attention regardless.

"Why aren't you married?" he asked suddenly, his eyes on the horse, not me. If I had been taken aback by his forthright nature earlier, this question nearly knocked me off my feet. Far too bold, yet I liked it. I rested my hand on his arm.

"I will be honest with you, Simon. Something I've not been with my previous suitors. My heart lies elsewhere, and I do not care to wed someone who doesn't have my heart."

Simon rubbed Zeus's snout. "The King? Prince-Bishop Werner?" he ventured. My heart skipped a beat, and I nodded.

"My apologies if you've been misled. My parents are trying hard to find me a match, no matter how fruitless the search."

"He's married, though, to the Queen Berta. How does your heart handle that?"

His questions! Had any man been this candid? Other than Werner had, that was . . .

I swallowed. How could I answer? Revealing the truth spoken by my mirror was not an option.

"I know. I'm pining, but I don't know any other way to be." My words were close to the truth.

At this, Simon turned, that soft gaze of his ensnaring me, intoxicating, and I had the drunken sense that if my heart wasn't so committed to Werner and my knowledge of his marriage's ultimate demise, I could be easily swayed by this man.

"Maybe you just haven't met the right person."

His words held a ring of truth, that I well knew. But the mirror vowed, and I wasn't going to give up on my heart's desire. Simon must have noticed my hesitancy, and he took both of my hands in his warm ones.

"How about this? We make no commitment. I will apply no pressure. You are still young and more beautiful than any woman I've ever met. And your honesty is shockingly refreshing." I had to bite my tongue at that. He continued. "Why don't I call on you, as a friend, and see if your heart can pry itself from your lost dream of the Prince-Bishop? I can only imagine how painful it was to lose the man you loved in such an improbable way. We will share each other's company and see what arises from that. What do you think?"

Speech fled from my lips. Simon was too kind. His softness was more than an outer skin — it permeated him to his core. In my head, I knew I should say no; my rigid affection wasn't fair to him. But he stirred something in my heart, something long locked away, and I found myself leaning into him and kissing his cheek.

"If nothing else, Simon, I would be honored to call you a friend. I don't think my heart can be swayed, but you are welcome to try."

His earnest eyes crinkled at the corners when he smiled. "I shall consider your acceptance of this offer the start of swaying your heart. Now," he said, holding his arm out to me, "we should find our way back to your dining hall, lest you parents think I absconded with you."

Simon's offer robbed me of my sleep, of my focus. Mother asked me where my head was several times the following day, and by the time I took my noon meal, which I didn't eat, I only pushed it around on my plate.

Mostly I wondered why he'd asked to court me. Such a handsome young man, he must have had his pick of available young women. Why had he sought me out? On nothing more than a wisp of hope?

The immediate answer was my money — or rather, my father's money. What other reasons could there be?

I nearly dropped my fork when it came to me. My mirror! This seemed like something my mirror would know. My mother's glare held me in quiet reprimand. No manners in dropping one's fork, after all.

"May I be excused mother? I'm not feeling myself."

At first, I thought she'd say no, but then her warm blue eyes softened at me. "Of course, darling.

You are looking a bit peckish. Why don't you lie down? Don't want to overwork yourself before Simon returns."

Ahh, there it was. Regardless of her conniving, I'd use Simon as an excuse this time to get out of lunch. Instead of lying down in my room, I fled the upper floors of the manse and descended into the cold darkness of my cellar.

I felt better almost immediately. The cool comfort of my cellar might not appeal to anyone else, but for me, the cellar exuded love and grace, and if I closed my eyes, I smelled my grandmother's oil for her dry skin, the wool of her skirts, the aroma of whatever potion she'd prepared that day. Now, with my mirror guarding the corner and my own spices and jars, it was as if my grandmother and I blended together. I felt as close as I could since her death.

I inhaled deeply, finding peace in the dusky, moldy scents, and tucked my hair up under my hood against the chill. Though the cellar was temperate in the summer, it was downright chilly in the winter. Sometimes, if the wind blew strong from the north, frost etched the stones on the north side wall. I then tucked the hood into my collar so only my pale white face was exposed to the elements.

My mirror was dark, asleep, but brightened with swirling smoke on the glass when I approached. The smoke ebbed and billowed on the glass until a semblance of a face formed. I grinned at the mirror.

"Magic Mirror, why does Simon Von Scuffer desire to woo me?" I wasn't going to be coy. Why bother? The mirror could read my deepest heart. Lying or hedging served no purpose.

"You, my Queen, are yet the fairest in the land."

I chewed at my lip and tapped my foot. That's it? While I was flattered to still be considered the grandest beauty in the land, I had hoped he'd seen more in me than just my skin.

"Any other reason?" I pressed.

The smoke swirled. "Von Scuffer's house is not as wealthy as the Baron's. That wealth might intrigue him as well."

That was believable. The pretty daughter of a wealthy man? I could have the personality of a rock and men would flock to me. Something about Simon though . . . Other men expected me to fall on my knees, grateful for their interest. They believed I'd swoon at any meager marriage offer.

Simon hadn't offered that, yet. He'd offered friendship first. A way to soften my heart perchance?

The reflection in the mirror caught my flashing eyes. My heart.

It still pined for Werner.

Though he was married and had a child, he also had my heart — the same heart Simon longed to claim as his own.

I chewed my lips more, until the wine-hued blood stained my lips in a grotesque make-up.

My eyes slowly shifted, rising to see the ancient, black-leather bound book high on its shelf.

One more spell. I'd risk it, that I knew like I knew every crevice of my cellar. I'd tried so many white spells, now I needed one more chance to be with Werner before I committed to Simon. And to make sure my heart opened to him the way it should. Echoes of Grandmother's long ago heartbreak spell sounded in my ears. What good would come of having Werner love me again if I couldn't love him back?

Almost as if I were mesmerized by the thought, my slender, long-fingered hand reached for that shelf — I had to stand on my tippy-toes to reach it. The book fell into my fingers as if it knew my intentions, and I brought it down, blowing on it to dislodge the caked-on dust. Unlike my other book, where white spells and potions were mixed with some darker ones that I had avoided since the catastrophe years ago, this book was heavy with the weight of only dark spells, as if the magic contained in the book added to the pages, making them thicker, heavier, more difficult to manage.

I hefted the book to my table and flipped the cover open. Another burst of dust. My eyes skimmed over the list of recipes, watering when they fell on the entry for the costly mistreatment spell, in search of something more. A love token or potion wouldn't work. I knew that because I'd tried a few when Grandmother wasn't looking and again when Werner first married Berta. Love tokens and potions weren't enough to break the bonds of marriage.

I knew not where Werner's heart lay. He had a daughter now — what if his love for his wife and child had grown and encapsulated the whole of his heart, like the thorny vines of the rose bush?

I'd need something stronger, something powerful to hack away at those vines so his heart might turn to me again. And only a black spell held such power.

My mirror watched in silent judgment as I searched for a recipe to unlock a captured heart. Once I found the one I thought might work, I busied myself on the potion and called out the words to the shadows of my cellar. The air popped and sizzled, smelling much like the air after lightning strikes an unfortunate tree. Tingling surged throughout my body, even to my hair and fingernails. In my head, the lone, singular image I focused on was of Werner, his hair like night and his eyes like the sunset, his strong arms reaching for me, and the rest of the world, my cellar, even the swirling of my mirror fell away. There was only Werner.

In that moment, I made a decision. If I were successful, then I'd gracefully decline Simon, accept whatever price the spell demanded, and wed the man of my heart. If not, I'd wed Simon, accept my lot, and be happy with him for the rest of my days.

Chapter Eight

SIMON WAS EARNEST in his offer. He came to the manse twice a week, and we strolled the gardens. Then, as the weather changed and snow capped the mountains and covered the towns, blanketing the houses and markets in a lacy white cover, we either bundled up to walk or enjoyed teacups of hot Swiss chocolate milk before the fire.

And every time, Simon maintained his distance, engaged me in conversation about books we've read, local news and gossip, and childhood antics. He kept me smiling for the entire meeting, and truly, I warmed to him. In another life, I could have easily fallen in love with him in a moment.

Were my parents ecstatic? Oh, I imagined my mother planning our summer wedding in her mind. She'd already dropped several hints and slyly asked if Simon had mentioned marriage at all.

My poor mother.

One afternoon in late January after sipping our chocolate, the sun burst from the clouds and the entire landscape shimmered in diamond dust. Simon tipped his head to the window.

"Should we take advantage of the beauty of the day and walk?"

We scrambled to wrap ourselves in our winter coats and gloves and made our way to the gardens.

"It is beautiful!" I exclaimed, whirling in circles amid the sparkling snowdrifts. Simon caught my arms and faced me.

"Not nearly as beautiful as you," he said in a husky voice that made my heart quiver in my chest. My blood surged in my body, warming me with sizzling excitement from the inside out.

Then, before I could move, he was kissing me, his cool lips fervent against mine. And oh save me, I was lost in that kiss. I placed my kid-gloved hand on his smooth jaw above his knitted scarf and kissed him back.

I'd only kissed Werner before, and that had been so long ago. This kiss was immediate, hot in the cold weather, and sent shivers all the way to my toes. I didn't want it to end.

Simon broke the kiss and pressed his forehead against mine. His breath was steamy against my face, and his hazel-brown gaze held my eyes, entrancing, captivating. Despite the conflict roiling inside me, I couldn't look away.

"Your heart," he whispered, "has it been swayed at all?"

I dropped my gloved hand to his chest made bulky by his wool coat. Maybe Simon and my parents were right. Maybe it was time for me to put my dreams of Werner to rest, lock them away, and never return. Simon made me happy. I could be content with him. And his kisses excited me. Maybe Simon was my new path. If the spell I'd cast hadn't turned Werner back to me, maybe it had opened my heart, just in a way I hadn't intended.

Maybe it opened my heart to Simon.

I flipped my hair over my shoulder and gave him a sly smile.

"I think you have swayed it, just a bit," I said coyly.

His own smile widened, and all bundled up as he was, his bulk reminded me more of a gentle bear than a soft doe. *My Simon.* Could I grow accustomed to that idea after so long thinking of *My Werner*? My chest throbbed as I gazed into his shining eyes.

Yes, maybe I could. His persistence had paid off.

He kissed me again, quickly this time. "Your eyes rival diamonds in this brilliant light, your skin clearer than the snow. I enjoy every moment I spend with you. You are all things bright and beautiful, and if it's amenable to you, I'd like permission to officially court you."

So formal! But the crinkle in the corner of his eyes told me he was teasing, if a bit. Still the lighthearted Simon, even in this heartfelt moment.

"Yes, but you'll have to ask my father for his permission before I can fully agree."

Simon's smile didn't falter at all. "I have no doubt that he'll grant his blessing. He was the one who invited me over that first night, after all."

A slight giggle bubbled inside me. When was the last time I'd giggled?

The only downside was how I was going to tell him about my secret cellar? Just as quickly as the idea entered my head, I dismissed it. I'd cross that bridge when I arrived at it.

Thinking on my cellar made me realize that, perchance in their own ways, my spells and chants had worked. Even this last dark spell, with no cost that I could yet determine. I had cast so many, asking for my true love — it never occurred to me that my true love, the love my mirror spoke of, was someone other than Werner.

Simon linked my arm with his. "Let's go back to your house and find your parents and share with them our good news."

We stomped snow off our boots before entering the rear hall and hung our dripping coats and gloves on the pegs by the door. I grasped Simon's hand, leading him to the salon where my mother would inevitably be basking in the sun, anticipating our return.

Instead of only my mother, my father also stood in the salon with another man whom I didn't recognize. Their faces sagged, heavy with whatever news this stranger had brought. For a moment, I had a flash to the last time I interrupted a similar scene, and I squeezed Simon's hand as my heart raced. Surely I wouldn't lose another suitor to foul news? My chest pounded in my throat, choking the words that struggled to emerge.

"Mother, what's going on? Who's this man?"

"Darling, please sit down. We've had some news."

"Mother, what news?"

My mother's lips thinned, then she gave me a tight smile.

"It's not as bad as all that. But we have to attend a funeral."

My brain froze as hard as my mother's garden statue in winter. Had Werner died? Was that why Simon had managed to thaw my frozen heart?

"Whose funeral?" Simon asked, his own voice strained. He yet held my hand, and it tightened, nearly crushing my fingers.

"Simon, you most likely have a message at your chateau as well. The Queen of Ula and Valais, the Prince-Bishop's wife Berta, has died of the coughing disease."

All the light seemed to evaporate from the salon, darkening everything but tiny pinpoints of light in my eyes, until I no longer saw the salon. Rather, my cellar appeared before me, my sweeping cape taking up residence and the echo of my voice chanting. It had been more than ten years, but the mirror had finally been correct. Berta had died and now Werner was free.

A moment of harsh realization struck my chest and stole my breath away. Had *I* done this? Was this the cost of the dark spell I'd cast months ago? Had she contracted the disease then?

Had my desire for Werner been paid in blood? A cost far too dear and I panted, trying to regain control of my thoughts.

In a far corner of my mind, I didn't care. My heart was iron against Berta. Then, I was almost more horrified that I didn't care that I might have killed her. Was that part of the cost, too? That my heart had hardened so much that I didn't have a care if my magic resulted in death? What if it had hardened against Werner as well?

No, I didn't think so. The price I'd paid was worth it. And to me, her death was worth any cost if it meant Werner's liberation. Then I turned my head slightly to gaze at the man beside me.

Simon stood next to me – real, holding my hand, ready, wanting me. Now, no waiting, no spells, just his whole heart. I had come to care for him dearly, so much that I was willing to consider his hand in marriage.

In truth, he was too good of a man for the likes of a callous, icy-hearted, witchy woman such as me.

I had no words. My wide-eyed silence spoke loud enough.

"We have to attend the canton funeral in three days," my mother's voice interrupted my dire thoughts and drew me back to the salon, now made less bright by the weight of the dismal news.

"Simon, I think —" I choked out.

The tension in his body forced the muscles in his neck to stand out. Everything about him appeared strained. He shook his head and bowed. "Say no more. Now is not the time. I must go home and see to my own message regarding the funeral."

Then he kissed my hand and released it, bowed curtly to my parents, and departed out the front door. The second the door snapped shut, my mother whirled around at me, her face harder, angrier than I'd ever seen in my life. She gripped my arms in her hands, clenching deep and painfully, ready to bruise me with her intensity.

"Don't think it, Adalee," she hissed. "You have a man right here, a wealthy, handsome man who wants to wed you as soon as he can. One who loves you despite all your flaws. You don't know what Werner is thinking or where his heart lays, or how long he will be in mourning. He probably doesn't think on you at all anymore! You were nothing more than a youthful indiscretion. As I told you years ago, forget Werner and focus on what you have, a strong, gentle man who wants you as you are right now."

Her sharp voice cut more deeply than a knife, tearing my insides to shreds, but she wasn't wrong. News of the queen's death brought all my desires for Werner crashing back harder than the waves of the sea, and the words of my mirror reverberated in my ears, drowning hers out.

A biting smack caught my cheek, a smack from my mother, lurching me from my thoughts. In a stupor, I raised my hand to my abused face. Her eyes burned with anger at me.

"Give up the dream of Werner, Adalee. I can see it in your face. Marry Simon and move on with your life. We are going to this funeral out of obligation, and that will be the last I want to hear of Werner in this house."

She stormed off, leaving my father and the stranger to stare at her with matching dumbfounded looks. I stood there like a fool, holding my cheek and blinking back tears. My father reached for me, but I couldn't stand it. My world seemed to be collapsing around me, and I raced for the one place where I might find some answers and succor for the heated chaos in my head.

The mirror

Before the Magic Mirror

.

Chapter Nine

ITS SCREEN WAS already smoky, swirling, prepared for the questions it knew I ached to ask. I threw myself at the elaborate frame, clinging to it — a woman sinking in a sea of unknown.

"Magic Mirror, what do I do? Is Werner now mine? Was Berta's death the price of my spell?"

Its reflection swirled, forming a visage to answer me.

"We all pay a price for our actions, my Queen."

Concise, enigmatic, but overt enough for me. The mirror's answer told me that, indeed, Berta had paid the ultimate price for my black spell. But the mirror had said "we all." I presumed that meant my own icy heart, now uncaring heart, was also part of that cost. I gritted my teeth, steeling myself for the question I had to ask next.

"Is this the moment, then? Is Werner coming for me? Are we to wed?"

The nimbus face shadowed the gleaming surface, and my throat tightened. What would it say? It spoke in riddles so often — would I be able to discern the mirror's meaning?

"Two choices present, two options collide. One is peace, the other chaos will provide."

Peace? Chaos? What did it mean? I shook the mirror frame in my quivering hands. Had one of my potions or spells caused Werner more pain? Was the chaos if I went with Werner, a result of the spell I'd cast? I had dabbled more and more in the black magic — was the mirror suggesting that I was to pay even greater of a price for my magic? When did the debt for that spell end?

"Mirror!" I yelled sharply, giving it another good shake. "What does that mean? Do I choose Simon or Werner? Just answer plainly!"

I couldn't believe I was asking about Werner. Maybe the mirror was pointing out the same thing my mother had — my foolishness in still pining for

Werner. He hadn't shown any interest in years, nor would he while in mourning. Was I expecting too much? Is that what the chaos meant? Or did he mean my heart would be in chaos if I chose Simon because I would always pine for Werner?

Sometimes I hated the mirror's enigmatic statements. And I hated it now.

"Mirror!" I yelled, again, my anger and frustration bubbling under my skin, popping to the surface in explosive fury. I rose up tall under my dark cape and glared at the mirror.

The mirror didn't answer. I wasn't thinking, not rationally at least, and I grabbed the closest thing I had — a heavy, silver apple-shaped paperweight, and I threw it at the mirror as hard as I could.

My aim was horrible. I threw poorly and the paperweight caught the edge of the gilt frame, chipping it. The reflective surface stilled, returning only my distraught image.

I crumpled to the threadbare rug, my velvet skirts flaring out around me. I had time, at least. I might be able to put Simon off for a few days. We had a funeral to attend after all, and that bought me time to see if Werner was still my soulmate as I had always thought him to be.

If not, then the choice was made for me.

The funeral was short, cold in the frigid air, and all of Valais and Ula made their drab appearance, it seemed. Though I held no affection for Berta, the pathetic woman who had stolen my love, a pang vibrated in my chest at a life of a mother cut short. Maybe my heart wasn't fully encased in ice and iron yet.

Her daughter stood next to my Werner, still as handsome and dark in his black cloak as the day we'd last kissed. I had hoped to catch his gaze, get a sense of where his heart might lay, but he kept his eyes lowered, as though no one else were standing in the snow with him. The pang in my chest throbbed ever harder at his sad countenance.

The daughter, however, appeared more interested in the funeral workings than her father. Rumors of her stark beauty were correct — indeed, the child, or young woman rather, was a doll. Her bright blue eyes stood out against her skin that was more pure white than the fresh snow on the hills. Her black hair, her father's hair, was so black it shone almost blue in the dusky sunlight. She had the type of beauty that she was unaware of, and a flare of hot jealousy coursed through my frozen appendages. Youth and beauty — she rivaled my own. And I was no longer young. Who wouldn't be jealous?

Her eyes were wide as she flicked them around the graveyard, from her mother's coffin to the drifts of snow, to those gathered in the crowd.

From under my black, fur-lined hood, I studied the girl, and when her bright eyes landed on me, I gave her a slight, reassuring smile. If she might be my stepdaughter, then I desired to make a strong impression on her.

Impressed or not, she narrowed her eyes, then twisted to her father and brushed flakes of snow from her brilliant red cape. No mourning black for the spoiled daughter of the king.

My parents and I didn't linger at the grave site, instead leaving as soon as the priest finished his short sermon and retreating to the carriage, then the warmth of our manse. I seated myself next to the blazing hearth with a book to try both to warm and occupy myself on this cold, dreary day.

"Simon tried to get your attention. Did you even say hello to him?" My mother's voice addressed me from across the room, startling me from my literary reverie.

"What? No, I didn't see him." I closed the book, marking my page with my finger. She had a bee in her bonnet, and she'd not stop talking no matter how much I ignored her. I resigned myself to her lecture that I knew was forthcoming.

"I know. You were too busy staring at the Prince-Bishop. I saw you. I saw what you were doing. Stop your girlish fantasies, Adalee! Simon is right here. He wants to marry you, which is a gift at your age."

I squinted a hard glare at my mother. "What does that mean?"

She pressed her palms together under her chin. "You aren't getting any younger. Your beauty will fade. You need to nab Simon while you still can. The king can have any woman in the land. What makes you think he's not going to choose a young, beautiful woman over you?"

"There is more to a woman than her beauty. Werner and I, we had something more."

She snorted. "You think? Maybe years ago, but not presently. No, powerful men like him, they want beautiful and young. You may still have your beauty, but your youth is slipping. And that beauty will be fleeting, soon enough. Marry Simon. He will assuredly be asking your father for his blessing soon. Say yes or find yourself alone for the rest of your life."

This must be what my mirror said with chaos — that my entanglements with Simon would cause me strife. Perchance this was the answer to the mirror's mysterious message.

I didn't respond to my mother — I stared her down until she grunted at me and returned to the kitchens. I flicked my eyes to the snow falling on the trees outside. My heart, more than my mind, made the decision.

If Werner came to me, I would say yes.

It just had to happen soon.

Before the Magic Mirror

Chapter Ten

SIMON CALLED ON me later that week. The snow had stopped, but ice danced in the frigid air in sharp, beautiful crystals. Even my black cloak, closed tightly around every exposed inch of skin, couldn't keep the cold from biting. I'd have rather entertained Simon inside by the fire. Yet he urged me outside, away from the prying gaze of my mother.

"The past week interrupted us," Simon explained as we walked the snow-brushed walkway.

Snow coated the bushes and trees surrounding us in great white monoliths, offering us a modicum of privacy. I tingled at his words, not from the cold, as I had a feeling where his conversation was going. And I wasn't ready for it.

"I want to move forward with you." He stopped and when I turned to him, his hands, clad in brown woolen gloves, grasped my cheeks, forcing my gaze to his. "I would ask your father for his blessing to marry you."

I opened my mouth to answer — with no idea of what words were going to form — when his warm lips found mine. He started softly, like rose petals in summer, but his kiss deepened, grew more aggressive, and a conflicting surge of desire and anxiety sparked deep in my belly. My body wanted his kiss, but my heart, it lingered elsewhere.

"Adalee?" A smooth voice carried over the icy landscape, a voice etched in my mind, one I heard every day it had been gone.

Werner.

I ripped my lips from Simon and stepped back as though I'd been caught doing something wrong. Wiping Simon's kiss from my mouth, I spun to see Werner cutting through the snowy bushes into the garden, sending patches of snow flying into the air, like he was emerging from a dream.

"Werner! What are you doing here?"

The pained expression that clouded his magnificent eyes cut my heart.

"I would have thought you'd know why."

I lifted my hand, as if to reach for Werner, but Simon grabbed it, spinning me to face him.

"What is this, Adalee? Why is the Prince-Bishop here?"

Considering Werner was his king, I was shocked at Simon's lack of respect. He didn't even acknowledge the Prince-Bishop's presence. I flicked my eyes from Simon to Werner. However, his question was the same one I had.

"Yes, Werner. Why are you here? Aren't you yet in mourning?"

His all-black dress, from his wool cap to his black wool redingote to his black breeches, cloak, and boots, he looked the part of the mournful widower, yet his behavior in searching me out here . . .

"Mourning, yes. As much as I can. You know it wasn't a love match, Adalee, and my side is empty without you. It's been empty for years. Now that I'm free, I want you. I've waited so long."

His words were pure bliss to my ears, and my heart soared to the heavens. Again, I opened my mouth to answer — this was it! The moment I had waited for, pined for, it was here! Simon, however, had other plans and stepped in front of me before any response could fall from my lips.

"You're too late. She's spoken for. We're going to be wed."

My astonishment at Simon's statement must have shown on my face. Werner leaned to his side to gaze at me around Simon.

"Is that true, Adalee? Am I too late?"

My mind spun in a dizzying whirl. Why was Simon lying — lying to his king? Was Werner really here in my gardens, asking for me before his time of mourning is done? Had the world turned upside down? What was real?

"No, you're not —" I started to say before Simon whirled on me. Those soft eyes blazed at me, no longer a doe but a wolf.

"Don't speak to him, Adalee. I'm speaking with your parents today. We will be wed."

I froze, unable to move at Simon's harsh words and biting tone. What had happened to Simon? My kind, gentle Simon? Why was he behaving so inappropriately, especially in front of the Prince-Bishop? I gathered my wits enough and shifted to step around him, but his hand snatched my arm in an iron grip. Whatever softness Simon had shown me in the past months was gone, and in his place stood a stranger. A fearsome stranger.

"Leave off her," Werner's stern voice broke through my shocked reverie. Then his hand was on Simon's, wrenching his hand from my arm. Simon spun on him and shoved Werner, who stumbled but managed to retain his feet.

Werner's face grew hard, and he inhaled, lifting his shoulders at Simon. In his black garb, he looked terrifying and powerful, and Simon must have realized the breach he'd committed against the king, for he bowed his head at Werner.

"My apologies. I forget myself." His voice was contrite. Yes, he *had* forgotten himself, pushing the king! What was he thinking?

"I think 'twould be best if you left," Werner commanded, leaving no room for argument.

Simon bowed slightly, and giving me a despairing glance, turned away and left the gardens. And with his departure, his offer of marriage left with him.

Werner's darkened visage shifted, calming, his candlelight eyes soft as he lifted them to me.

"You came," I told him in a marveled voice.

My mirror might have predicted it, and though my spell casting skills had grown, I hadn't truly believed it would happen. After so many years, who would? Yet, here we were, together, alone in the garden after so many years. My entire body shook at this moment.

"I promised you that you were my soulmate. Having to wed another against my will wasn't going to stop that. Only delay it a little." His full lips curled on one side. Had he too doubted our reunion?

"But you're in mourning! Won't this look a bit untoward?"

Why was I asking such a thing? This moment was the one I had craved — and now I was hesitant? Worrying about appearances? I should be throwing myself at him. A sudden memory of my grandmother's potion that might have hardened my heart hard rang in my head. Had that happened? Or had the cost of my own dark spells been paid with my icy heart? Did my heart no longer call for him?

Werner took my gloved hands in his own.

"Maybe, but as Prince-Bishop, I can bend the rules. And I have already waited too long for you to be my Queen."

Then he leaned forward and pressed his lips on mine. The past fourteen years fell away in a rush, and I was a young woman back in the fall garden, kissing him as I had when we were betrothed. He pulled his head back and cupped my cheek with his woolly hand.

"The only thing is, I do have a daughter. We will have to take some time for her to get to know you. Can you accept my daughter as your own?"

I placed my hand over his. I'd had my reservations about his daughter, affectionately named Sella, after witnessing her hard eyes study her mother's funeral, but I would do my best with her. That was all I could promise. If necessary, I'd concoct a potion to heal any breach that might arise between us.

"She will never have the thought that her home is not her own. And if God is willing, she will have a gaggle of brothers to entertain her as well."

He kissed me again, then grasped my hand and led me back to the manse to inform my parents of our good news.

To say our joyful news was not well received was an understatement. My parents bemoaned the quick actions of the king and reminded me of my interest in Simon. *What of his poor heart?* they inquired. Werner pointed out that Simon was a wealthy enough young man and that he would find another to love. Werner vowed to make that one of his own personal intentions, to help find a bride to quell Simon's emotional toil.

However, I knew of a wonderful potion that would work far more quickly to help find Simon a wife and soothe his broken heart. Thus, I silently vowed to spend the next day not celebrating my reunion with Werner, but in my icy-cold cellar with my cape over my head, concocting the perfect potion to help Simon forget his desire for me and find another woman who would love him the way he deserved to be loved.

My mother pursed her thin, white lips at Werner's promise, an expression I had grown unpleasantly familiar with, but she said nothing. She was in the presence of royalty, after all, and her daughter was to become Queen — what could she say? Nothing. It was difficult not to grin at her discomfiture.

Simon sent me a note before I departed my parents' home, apologizing for his poor behavior and wishing me all the best. I clutched the letter to my chest. He was truly a decent man, and I wished him all the best in return. It was the least he deserved for how well he handled my sudden change of heart.

The citizens of Valais gossiped like schoolchildren about Werner's rush to marry again. Oh, how rumors abounded. Some were even downright vile! But those rumors died down quickly enough. Werner's citizens seemed forgiving of their mourning king.

My biggest concern now was what to do with my cellar. I needed everything in that hidden underground sanctuary, and I needed it moved to the castle with as little fanfare as possible. My new husband must never know of my rather unorthodox hobby.

Werner had been generous with his purse before we wed, so I removed several coins and found two gruff men in the village. They helped me wrap all the belongings in the cellar, and with an extra silver to ensure their silence, they moved it all secretly to another abandoned dungeon-esque room I had already selected in the castle. I knew they'd keep their mouths shut, if not for the coin, then for a possible curse I might cast upon them with if they mentioned my secret.

I made sure they knew *that* as well.

One of the men, a burly fellow with dirt-encrusted nails, winked as he left and told me to call on him again if need arose. He had mentioned he was a huntsman, able-bodied and capable of using every measure of tool and weapon. I eyed the man, his scruffy brown hair and thin beard, his thick shoulders and legs that fairly resembled a gigantically stout Belgian Draft horse I'd seen once at a royal event. He seemed a man who prided himself on his ability to take on the lowliest of tasks.

Though I nodded at him, I gathered my hood close to my chin, hoping that would never be the case.

Once they departed, I stood in the center of the dungeon, now my cellar, and turned in a slow circle, taking it all in. The abundance of cobwebs and musty smell told me the space hadn't been used in decades, perchance longer, and it would serve my purpose exactly.

The only change I had to make was to find a space for my beloved magic mirror. Though Werner had gifted it to me, with the enchantment upon it, I couldn't very well hang it in my bedroom that I now shared with Werner. Oh, what he might think if he saw me speaking to a glass! Instead, I relegated it to the new cellar. I made sure to give it a place of honor, right next to the blackened, narrow hearth on a fine copper stand.

On my second day in the castle, while Werner was buried in his study and the servants prepared for our upcoming wedding, I descended into the dungeon and removed the black cloth from the mirror. I hadn't spoken to it in a week, and the time had come to start using it again. Now that I was a queen, I needed my mirror's counsel more than ever.

"Magic Mirror on the wall, who's the fairest of them all?"

"You are, my queen," the swirling face answered.

I smiled.

Everything in my life was as it should be.

Everything that was, except for Werner's daughter, Sella.

The sun managed to push past the gray clouds and shine on my cold wedding day. Our late-winter wedding was a simple one. Werner had sent word to the local dressmaker, who quickly tailored a rich, dove-gray brocade into a stunning gown that flattered my dark hair and silvery eyes. Even my mother gasped when she saw me in it. Not quite the red gown from my youth, but a stunning, more mature bride about to become royalty.

"Fit for a queen," she commented, her eyes glistening. I kissed her cheek, grateful she found her peace in my rash decision to wed Werner.

My father, looking rather dapper in a black velvet redingote coat that fit his much more trim frame, held my hands in his. He didn't speak, but gazed at me with proud, tearful eyes before kissing my other cheek and readying himself to take me to the church where Werner awaited.

Our wedding was a flourish of color and celebration. While nobles and barons might have grumbled at our rush to wed, I ignored them and instead delighted in the cheers of those who were happy for us. Werner's daughter, Sella, was one of the grumbling sorts, and she sat with her arms crossed over her cobalt and yellow gown, and her lips a rose bud pout. She never left her padded chair in the corner of the hall, and after our luscious feast of pheasant, beef, nuts, fruits, and such a variety of breads and pastries that threatened to collapse the smorgasbord table, Werner dismissed her.

"I'd not lay eyes on her scowling face any longer on my wedding day," he'd told me with a subtle grin.

I didn't care either way. My exuberance was a sheet covering me the whole day, so I only saw happiness and joy. My heart hardened against everyone else who didn't share in that joy. Werner and my marriage to the man I'd loved my entire life was my singular focus that day.

Werner and I spent most of the days following our wedding locked in his bed chambers at Seta Castle. And I reveled in it! Finally, all those girlish dreams I'd clung to and believed to be gone forever resurfaced and came true. I was, indeed, the most fortunate of women. My Werner was in my arms once more, and I was his queen.

Sometimes, dreams really do come true.

Once the celebrations ended and we emerged from our chambers as newlyweds, Werner and I started our married life. He'd given me *carte blanche* to run the household as I saw fit. I gave him a sultry smile and started making plans. The solar, where I'd spent the past few days, was dingy, too dark for a room with such tall windows. Who had decided to drape them in heavy, dark fabric?

Those would be the first to go, and I said as much to Werner. His smile faltered as his golden eyes held my gaze.

"That is all well and good. But Sella spends an awful amount of time in that room, trying to connect with her mother who'd sewed there most days. Berta made those very drapes. But it should be fine."

I continued to smile at Werner, but my insides bubbled hotly at his words. Why would someone sew in so dark a room? Surely bright light would have been more suitable. Perchance his old wife didn't have a fair hand at sewing. Those dreary drapes attested to that. As for Sella, she'd have to learn, as I did, that life is nothing if not a series of changes.

"I'll be kind when I break the news to her, and she can even help me select new, lighter fabrics."

Werner cupped my neck and leaned in close to me, pleased at my suggestion to include Sella in the process. My heart leapt in my chest at his very presence.

"You are the kindest, most caring woman I know," he whispered huskily before kissing me.

Sella, on the other hand, wasn't as convinced of my plan as her father. She didn't want to help, scowled at me as I spoke, and when I was done, her watery blue eyes blazed with enmity.

"You can try to change the curtains," she told me in an insolent tone.

I raised a sleek eyebrow at her. What did that mean? Before I could ask, she whirled around and exited the solar.

Later that day, I asked the maid to send for the drapery seamstress. The maid nodded, but nothing came of my request. When I still hadn't seen the seamstress several days later, I inquired with the maid. The woman shrugged casually as she wiped down the mantle.

"Sella found me shortly after and told me that she and her father decided to keep the draperies. So I never sent for her."

My mouth twisted up at her words. "Well, I gave you a command. Since I am the queen and in charge of this house now, you defer to me, not to Sella."

The maid shrugged again. "But her father is the Prince-Bishop, and she said that he decided we keep them."

I had to tamp down the raging anger inside me that churned like a storm. "I understand, but the king has given *me* permission to make changes. Not Sella. So, the drapery seamstress?"

The maid dropped her arm to her side. "Unless the Prince-Bishop requests it, you'll have to wait. I don't want to go against his dictates."

"They are not his dictates!" I yelled, losing myself. Then I stiffened and patted at my hair, regaining my composure. Screaming was not becoming on anyone, least of all me. I gave the maid a tight, mocking smile as I looked down my nose at her. "I'll speak to Werner."

She nodded and exited the room in a rush.

But would Werner give in to me? Or would he make decisions to appease his spoiled, willful daughter? As much as that description seemed harsh, I had noted those traits in her over the weeks I lived in the castle. It was then that I realized what my problem was and what my life was going to be like with Werner.

That interaction with the maid was my initiation into what I deemed as Sella's habit. In the company of the servants, her governesses, and her father, Sella pretended to be the most dutiful, obedient daughter. She blossomed under their care, transforming into a divinely beautiful young woman, full of smiles and song. Sella even helped the servants in the kitchens with their baking and the house maids with the cleaning.

But alone, she was a different young woman altogether. I didn't miss the narrow, dark glares that she gave me when she passed me in the hall. She tried to keep Werner busy when he wasn't occupied with affairs of state, clinging to his side so I rarely had a moment alone with my husband. Whenever I tried to make a change in the house — to the mealtime menu, to the cleaning schedule, to the flowers planted in the gardens, she countered me, putting it all back to what it had been before I arrived, claiming it was what her father wanted.

She was quite the conniving one. And no one saw it but me.

Once she even took to scrubbing the stones outside my own personal salon when I'd asked the gardener to stain them a brighter color! She hadn't found him in time to stop his handiwork, and he managed to stain them all a beautiful cream. In retribution, she got on her hands and knees herself to scrub away my change. I stood in the library, wrapped in my lush black-velvet cape, and watched her with a flat expression. Let her stain her skirts scrubbing. I wouldn't permit her to know her behaviors, her very presence irritated me.

On the outside, she appeared the down-to-earth princess. Yet, she did it only as a means to strike at me. Though she may have been a blooming beauty, to me, it seemed her heart was as black as obsidian. She was a sharp stone in my shoe, an annoying one I couldn't get rid of.

I could see it, and no matter how many potions I concocted to soften her to me, to change her heart from black to loving, none of them worked. Over the months, as winter gave up its icy grasp to spring, I was running out of patience, losing my joy. What happened to my childhood dreams? They were all being dashed away by one selfish girl. I kept my wounded pride to myself — Werner had too much on his mind already. He didn't need me adding to those concerns, especially with regards to his beloved daughter. Plus, I was certain that once I had children, giving her needed siblings, her selfish nature would no longer be tolerated amongst the household.

So instead, I focused on Werner and myself when we were alone, living in those moments that meant the world to me. In our bed chambers, there was no lost time, no separation, no invasive daughters, only Werner and me alone.

One night, he came late to our chambers, offered me a spring rose he'd selected from the garden, and kissed my cheek in his way that sent shivers down my spine and made my toes curl. Had any woman so loved a man? No, only Werner and I loved to these heights.

Then he spoke the most innocent phrase, not knowing how it was a knife twisting in my heart.

"Sella is growing into such a beautiful young woman. She looks so much like her mother. I wouldn't be surprised if she rivals your own beauty one day, my love."

He kissed my cheek again, which felt like skin to his lips, but to me was as hard as stone. I hadn't expected him to make such a statement after all the lauding he'd remarked about my own beauty. My beauty was unrivaled, uncontested! It had even been the focus of some of the rumors swirling about our marriage! He had pride in his daughter, yes, but to compare her pasty looks to mine?

I gave him a false smile and joined him for bed. All I wanted was Werner's love, and here I was, in my own chambers, playing a distant second to a young woman who was ungrateful for all she had. I pushed his comment from my mind as we joined under the covers.

But later, as he snored, I fumed. Sella was turning everyone in my life against me and doing it so quickly! What was happening to this dream that I'd clung to for the whole of my life? Everyone cheered the beauty and grace of Sella while I lurked in the shadows, commander of my cellar only. Wasn't *I* the queen? Wasn't the castle staff supposed to cater to *me*? Wasn't Werner supposed to come to me and take my desires into consideration, put me before all others like he vowed at our wedding?

I seethed at Werner's statement that night, tossing and turning in bed. After Werner fell asleep, I wrapped myself in my black cloak and retreated toward my cellar to seek counsel with my mirror. My heart was heavy, weighted like a stone, as I closed the door on my snoring king.

It wasn't that I didn't like Sella. I loved her, if only for Werner's sake. I'd also understood this transition might take time. How much time? That I didn't know. I also knew Sella was getting older and must find her own place in the world. As much as I hated myself for thinking it, I wanted her to find that place so her beauty and presence didn't further usurp my place in Werner's heart and home. How could he love me if his daughter grew into a fierce beauty who continually reminded him of his dead wife?

That idea was too much for me to bear. Something must be done — something that would benefit me and Sella while still making my Werner happy. I had no answers, no solution. My mirror, on the other hand . . .

Since marrying Werner and moving my belongings into the dungeon, I hadn't visited my cellar as often as I liked. Not since I'd tried the spells to open Sella's had I retreated to my books. And when I did enter my cellar, it was solely to consult my mirror, not concoct any potions or make any spells. My life was nearly perfect! What need had I for spells? My mirror might be able to tell me.

The mirror stood as a dark and silent sentinel in the chilly dungeon. I had cleaned the space as much as I could, but too soon, the webs and musty smell returned. I was learning to ignore it and focus on my purpose. Pushing my draping sleeves up my arms, I stood before the mirror, waiting for its smoky reflection to form.

"Magic Mirror, who's the fairest of them all?" I whispered. I needed its validation.

"You are, my queen," it responded without pause. The words, however, brought only momentary relief as the mirror continued. "But the princess of snow white skin will claim that title soon."

What? Not Sella! I froze, studying the murky mirror face. *Not my mirror, too!* Who else was set to turn on me?

"I've tried to be kind to her," I lamented to my mirror. "To be the mother she lost, but she insults me at every turn. My heart is weary from her. I have yet to quicken with my husband's babe, and I feel like I am all alone here. What can I do with this girl who has turned my entire house against me?"

The mirror was silent for a time, the smoke swirling in response. Then the face brightened.

"Her presence will bring you and Werner pain. And if she leaves, she does not have to return."

I narrowed my eyes at the mirror. The statement sounded deplorable to my ears. Not return? Maybe I had misunderstood.

"You mean, a boarding school? Send her away to be a royal maid somewhere else?"

More smoke. I waited patiently, chewing my lips bloody.

"The girl enjoys her exploration of the woods, in being away from the keep. She does not have to return."

I gasped, clutching my cape tight against my face and neck.

What was it saying? Surely my mirror meant sending her away to school. Otherwise, why would my mirror suggest such a thing? That was black magic he spoke! The darkest of black magic, to rob one of life! When had my mirror started to dabble in those darker tones?

When had it started to reflect me? My inner thoughts and desires?

I threw the black sheet back over it, as if hiding the reflective surface I might hide its hideous suggestion and raced back to bed.

Before the Magic Mirror

Chapter Eleven

But the idea of sending Sella away swelled within me as months passed. I couldn't stop thinking of it, of a way she might leave and return once her education was complete, once she'd matured, and perchance even married. Then she'd never return. That *had* to be what my mirror intoned. And I *had* to discuss Sella's departure with Werner — she was getting worse every day.

At supper one evening, she distracted the servants, engaging them in banter as I tried to have them serve Werner and I. Sella waved a pasty white hand toward her father, gesturing for the kitchen maid to serve him soup. The maid's smile remained plastered on her face as Sella giggled and regaled them with tales of the wee bird she'd found and brought home, and the maid forgot to fill my bowl.

I flicked my eyes at Werner, but his attention remained fixed on Sella's smiling face as she continued to talk about her dumb bird. Pursing my lips, I tapped my spoon against my bowl, but the sound was drowned out by laughter at Sella's bird imitation.

Something inside my head burst.

That was it — the final straw. I wasn't going to be ignored in my own home.

I rose in a fluid movement, lifted my red and black brocade skirts, and stomped out of the dining room. I doubted I'd be missed.

Werner found me later that night as I read by the fire.

"What happened at supper, love?" he asked, kissing the top of my head. Using my finger to save my page, I closed the book on my lap.

"If you had managed to pull your attention from Sella and the maids, you might have noticed that I wasn't eating."

"What?" Werner stood up straight, cutting a fine figure in his black waistcoat. "Why not?"

"The maid was too busy being entertained by Sella to do her job and neglected to serve me soup."

Werner patted my hand as though this was a one off. "Well, I'll speak to the maid. It won't happen again."

"That's not true, Werner. This isn't the first time." My voice was flat, tired of Sella's games.

Werner pulled a high-back chair next to me and clasped my free hand in his.

"What do you mean, not the first time?"

I sighed. This was the moment I had dreaded, but if my mirror was right, I needed another option. Something that would make us all happy.

"Have you noticed that I'm treated like an outsider here, or worse, like I don't exist? The housemaids ignore my orders, the kitchen maids take my meal choices and toss them in favor of Sella's requests, and I am regularly forgotten at meals and bedtime. Everything in this house revolves around Sella."

"She has been here her whole life. It's natural for her to command the servants and for them to listen to her. She is just trying to lose herself in what is familiar since she's lost her mother. They will learn to follow your command soon enough."

I disagreed, but I bit back that comment. And once again, my heart wanted to bleed for the girl losing her mother. The girl's behavior, though, made that difficult. Surely it had to be more than the loss of a parent causing her outlandish behavior?

"Sella is getting older," I continued. "Her education should be seen to. She's been coddled here. Have you considered a school? She is royalty, and I believe she would benefit from that."

Not my idea, nor the mirror's. Rather, a common occurrence. Nobility often sent their sons and daughters away to school. I had escaped a boarding school education because my nanny had also been a brilliant governess, and my parents adored her too much to let her go.

Sella, however, manipulated her governess. I had been shocked to see how her basic educational needs had been dismissed, and she a princess who would one day marry a royal! Sending her to school was a solution that benefited her as much as it might me. Now was as good a time as any to rectify it.

"Send her away?"

Werner's voice wavered. I leaned close to him and cupped his cheek with my palm

"I know it seems drastic, but it's common for royalty, and you know that. You were sent to school, as were your siblings. You want her to be fit for her station, don't you?"

Ahh, there it was. Pride and position. Better than any magic. If nothing else, Werner believed in adhering to certain standards, and an educated princess of the Prince-Bishop was one of those standards.

He nodded slightly before lowering his head. "You are right, as always, my love. It should have happened sooner. We shall speak to her about it on the morrow. The *Chateau du Provence* is best. She should be there."

It was almost too easy, yet Werner didn't appear overly convinced. I needed to change that. Sella might have had her father wrapped around her finger, but I knew Werner's heart.

More importantly, this way it didn't end with endangering Sella or her not coming home.

The moment I entered the cool air of my cellar, my mirror started to swirl as if welcoming me, the black cloth covering having fallen to the stone floor. I swept in, the hem of my cape dragging against the stones, sweeping dust and cobwebs to the side. The table was cluttered with papers held in place by my silver apple paperweight, ornate candle holders, and other accoutrements of my potions and spells that I'd neglected to put away—scattered crumbs and globs of vitriol, pestles and goblets. I hadn't needed any to concoct anything in quite a while.

Until now. With Sella. For her, I didn't want
to rely on Werner's weak agreement to send her to
school. Why would I, when I could take matters into
my own hands and achieve the outcome I desired?

The more I thought about Werner and Sella
and our predicament, the more worked up I became
until sweat dripped under my cape and down my
temples, even in the chilled air. Though I hadn't
called on it, my mirror awoke and started to swirl,
disturbed by my reckless movements in the cellar.
Yet, it must have sensed my rising frenzy, for it said
nothing.

My main recipe book sat closed on the
copper book stand. Aged, beloved, the book my
grandmother had used exclusively. Full of bright
magic, with only a few lesser-dark magic spells and
potions littering the pages, spells that she and I had
avoided.

For the most part.

But those lesser spells weren't the type of
dark magic that mattered. Sure, they might incur a
low cost, but the spells weren't the ones that made
huge shifts to a person, that created dynamic change
or came at with significant debt. I scanned them
anyway, hoping a lighter potion or spell might work.
If I could avoid the debt, why not at least try.

A Shielding spell? A Protection potion? A
Warding Off incantation?

No, and I hadn't expected to find a spell that would work in that book. I wiped my forehead with a draping sleeve as I slammed the book shut. I was feverish, as if consumed by an illness. No illness, no sickness, only fevered by the desire to find the best solution that might send Sella away for a while. Now that I had an idea, a solution, my insides burned. I thought my bowels were melting.

I gripped the edge of the table, my long fingers digging into the soft, wooden surface, and I dropped my chin to my chest. What? What could I do to ensure Werner sent Sella to school, and more importantly, that she left the castle?

It had to be a spell, a powerful banishment spell. That was the only option. One that convinced Werner to send Sella away to *Chateau du Provence*. Only then would Werner and I be free to celebrate our love the way we should, unencumbered. I wasn't getting any younger, and I didn't want to waste the few years I had left of my youth competing with his daughter for Werner's attentions.

And going away to school was the best for her. That was what I told myself, *lied* to myself, in justification. That I was doing all this for Sella.

Time was of the essence. Not wasting it on light spells or potions that might take weeks or months to work, if they worked at all. No, a real spell, a true potion, one that couldn't be undone and would take effect immediately. I reached for the ancient book, the one I hadn't touched since I'd cast the dark spell to win back Werner.

The book of black magic had worked effectively then, so perfectly, barring his wife's death, of course. I assumed nothing less than perfection this time.

I replaced my everyday book on the book holder with the decrepit tome and scanned the list of recipes. My finger landed on the perfect one, a recipe to banish an irritation.

That's exactly what Sella is, I told myself as my lips curled up to one side. *An irritation.*

Did the spell mean a person? I shrugged. A bug or a rash or Sella, they were all irritations, at least to me.

Did that make me ruthless? Had my heart truly become a block of ice when it came to Sella? Perchance. And that was the price *I* paid for my spell to win Werner. I had to accept the cold savagery of my frozen heart and move on — but I could only move on with Werner and Werner alone.

My mirror finally came to life, and for the first time since I owned it, gave me a cautionary message.

"My queen, with the dark nature of this final step, you may lose what remains of your heart."

I grabbed the black cloth covering. "I don't have any heart left," I bit out and tossed the cloth over the mirror.

As much as I hated to admit it, I knew I was a full witch by this point. How could I be anything else after all I'd suffered? Grandmother might purse her thin, wrinkled lips at me, but she wasn't here, and I had skills that could be put to good use. As long as I controlled them, didn't abuse my powers, then what difference did it make if I were a witch or not? I was the queen – if anything, those skills only helped me be the best queen for Werner and our canton.

Now I was going to use those skills and create the future I desired.

The potion mixture was horrendous, and the addition of bubbling vitriol made the potion thoroughly dangerous. Green-gray smoke effused from the ornate chalice, and as I lifted it over my head, a rank, acrid cloud surrounded my head and made it swim.

Though I considered myself a witch and had crafted dark potions and spells before, something about this spell made my skin crawl and hand vibrate as I offered up the cursed chant. A little, oft-unheeded voice in my head told me I was taking this all too far, yet I ignored it. I cried out at the sensation, and my grip on the chalice loosened before I shifted my hands for a better grip. Breathing shallow through my mouth, I steeled myself against the power of the spell. That spiraling vibration started in my fingers again, and this time I welcomed it, let it become part of me. I'd need all my power to make this spell work.

Then the chalice exploded in my hands, and I cowered under my hood, shielding myself from the flaming contents. The drops landed, sizzled, and burned out. When I peeked around the edge of my hood, my cellar was dark, cool, calm, with only the flickering of candlelight breaking the stillness.

Had it worked? I studied my hands, which had fortunately escaped getting burned when the chalice broke. The droplets left black scorch marks on the old wooden table and the stone floor. I gathered the pieces of chalice and set them in a bin by the fire to dispose of later.

For now, my spell was done, and my mirror remained silent. It was time for me to rejoin Werner.

And wait for the spell to take effect.

I waited for evidence of the spell's effectiveness and Werner to talk with the girl about her future elsewhere, but he was called away to a problem in the south of the canton later that day, so he directed the task to me. It seemed perfect timing as I'd only cast the spell the night before, and here it was — the opportunity to speak to Sella about her upcoming departure.

Excitement bloomed in my chest like a fiery rose. Oh, but the spell worked more quickly than I'd expected if we were telling her the very next day! And at what cost? None that I could see. Perhaps the loss of the young woman from the household was a dear enough price to pay. Werner and the house maids would surely mope around the castle at first, but they'd soon adjust.

After a brief peek in my bedroom mirror to touch up my lip stain and tuck away a curly chestnut lock, I fluffed my skirts — a cream and blue lawn — and descended the stairs.

Sella hummed under her breath as she cleaned out the bird cage in the salon, a shockingly filthy chore. I had been surprised that Sella committed to doing it all herself instead of asking a housemaid to do it. What princess dirtied her hands in such a manner? Yet another reason the servants adored her. And another reason she needed the education suitable for a royal. *The girl must learn her place!*

Spring sunshine poured through the cut glass windows, bathing her a golden light, and it was easy to see why the mirror compared her beauty to mine, though I was loath to admit it. The girl was stunning, with shiny black hair that reflected blue-black in the light and her skin a pale-bright instead of her regularly pasty white. I had denied her fair looks for far too long.

Thank goodness she was leaving.

"Sella," I called out, breaking her sing-song work. She turned to me, and I was certain I noticed her smile falter before she plastered it back on.

"Hello, Mother Adalee," she responded in a cloyingly sweet voice, closing the door to the bird cage to keep the fluffy-headed budgies contained. "What can I do for you?"

Here she was, trying to ply that sweet girl act on me. It wouldn't work. I inhaled and steeled myself against her honeyed words.

"Sella," I tried again, "I must speak to you. Your father has asked it. Will you come sit with me?"

I perched on the settee, smoothing my skirts, and patted the cushioned seat next to me. She shrugged and joined me. Her frail frame barely took up any space on the overstuffed seat. How did someone so dainty cause so much trouble?

I took her bony hand in mine — her skin was so pale it was translucent and showed every blue vein like a map of the roads out of Lucerne. Oh, the poor child. Had she been sickly as a child? Werner hadn't mentioned such a thing. Suddenly I wondered if I had been mistaken in reading her. Was she ill like her mother had been? Werner hadn't said anything about it. Maybe she feared change, and her mother's death had made her physically ill? Keeping the house as it was must remind her of her mother. Maybe she saw me as an interloper and couldn't adjust to that change?

As I gazed down into her pale, rounded face, my normally icy heart tugged in my chest for her. So much loss, even for a princess who'd been given so much. But she was becoming a young woman, and her training and future were at stake. While she may not have liked me, I loved her father and cared for her enough to want her future to be set. In my heart of hearts, I truly wanted only the best for this wan little lady. And if it meant her leaving, so much the better. Everyone wins.

"Your father and I have been discussing your future."

Sella sat up tall — tall for her at least. "My future? What about my future?"

"Oh, dear, don't get worked up. It's good news for you. As the Prince's daughter, it is time for you to finish your schooling, to prepare yourself to be a Swiss Queen when the time comes to marry your own Prince-Bishop. Your father and I have selected the perfect school, the *Chateau du Provence*. Many royals send their children there." I kept my voice light, excitable through my wide smile, trying to encourage her excitement about this news.

She raised one raven-wing eyebrow at me. Oh, but she was quite the beauty — her father and my mirror weren't wrong. Her black hair curled softly around her face, flattering her smooth skin, framing her brilliant blue eyes and puckered lips that were as red as the roses in the garden. Then that beautiful face transformed to more of a scowl.

"A Swiss Queen. Like you, I suppose?"

I gave her a thin, matronly smile. "Well, not necessarily like me —"

"No, nothing like you," she spat out, her face hardening in front of me, twisting her lovely features. "My mother was a queen. You're just some trollop my father married before he even finished mourning. You are nothing like a queen!"

I dropped her hand and clasped it to my chest. Where had she learned such language?

"Sella! Watch your tone!"

She shot to her feet and glared at me with all the fury she daren't show her father or the servants. "No, I won't! I want nothing to do with you! And I won't leave my father alone with a leech like you! I'm not going anywhere!"

"Sella!" I cried and tried to reach for her kirtle, but she whirled from my grasp and raced out the back doors, grabbing her red cape from its peg by the door as she ran. Most likely she was heading for the woods just beyond the flower gardens, her favorite escape.

I wanted to race after her, but I stayed inside the keep. Her dislike for me had only grown into an ugly obstacle, and in her fury, she wouldn't accept any comfort from me. Best to let her throw her little temper tantrum.

Standing at the door, I watched her yellow skirts flash amongst the blooming trees as she ran deeper into the woods, far beyond the gardens, and I had a sudden new worry. What if she were so upset, she ran too far into the forest, beyond the bounds of the castle? What if she got lost, or encountered a dangerous animal? If her good sense was impaired by her emotion and she didn't pay attention to her surroundings? How would we find her and bring her home?

My mind spun, trying to figure out what to do. What had gone wrong? Werner didn't need to worry about his daughter after all his loss. What if her running away was the spell taking my desire for Sella to leave too far? The mirror had predicted she might run away into the woods! And now here she was, doing it!

No, I'd been precise, specific in my potion and curse. This wasn't the spell dispatching her. This was just an upset young woman running off because she didn't like being told she was going away to school soon. Spoiled, as always.

She'd explored most of the woods and knew them as well as she knew the castle grounds, so the mirror's prediction wasn't surprising. She wouldn't get lost. I sighed, my shoulders sagging. I'd give Sella time to cool her anger, and we'd resume the discussion when she returned, I vowed to myself.

She was going somewhere, no matter how much she protested.

Sella just needed some time.

When she didn't return later in the afternoon, the servants commented on her absence and my worry increased. It was nearing dusk and the shadows cast by the trees grew long on the ground. She'd never been gone this length of time, and especially not when her father was due home soon. My mind throbbed in a rush. What if she *were* lost? I couldn't focus. The words of my mirror echoed painfully in my brain. There had to be a solution. I needed a way to find her.

I ran down to the dungeon, my shoes slipping on the damp stairs. I grabbed at the sides of the stairwell so I didn't fall to my death. My magic mirror leaned against the wall, covered and forgotten. I flipped the cloth off its ornate frame. It had watched my frenzied spell casting with ominous silence. Now I needed it to speak.

"Magic Mirror on my wall, how can I find Sella? She's lost!"

The smoky, translucent face appeared in the center of my reflection. It spoke slowly, in a low guttural voice.

"Sella is lost yet might return. If you send your huntsman, your strife when she returns will end."

The strife would end — did it mean she'd come back from her tantrum in the woods? And the huntsman? What huntsman? Who was that? Again with the enigmatic proclamations! Who was the mirror talking about? For all my powers, I felt perplexed and useless. What good were my powers if they didn't give me command over something as minor as a runaway girl? I gripped the edge of the mirror, shaking it.

Then it came to me — the dirty-fingered stout man who'd moved my magic items to the dungeon! He'd mentioned he was a huntsman. I could pay him to track her down, and if necessary, drag her home if danger loomed. Brilliant! Leaving the mirror exposed, I raced back to my room.

I grabbed my black satin satchel, slipped the loop around my wrist, and rushed to the stables where the stable hand, Hans, scrambled to ready the carriage and take me to town.

My memory served me well, and I found the man at the Horn tavern. I asked Hans to bring him outside, as there was no way I was going demean myself and set foot in that dingy watering hole. I was a queen — I had a reputation to uphold.

The man stumbled outside and squinted in the bright sunlight. I waved Hans back to the carriage.

My hood tightened around my perfectly oval face as I lifted my head high. "My good sir, do you recall who I am?"

He peered down his nose at me and scratched at his filthy-looking beard.

"The queen with the peculiar books in the cellar. Yeah, I remember you."

I swallowed hard but kept the austere expression on my face. With the grimy man now standing before me, this seemed less and less like a sound idea.

"I have a job for you. My husband's daughter has raced off into the woods. Normally she doesn't go very far and just chases the animals, but I fear I might have angered her, and she's gone farther in than I feel is safe and has yet to return. This is very unlike her. She might be in danger or lost. I would like you to track her and bring her home."

The man's dark eyes studied me, much sharper than I expected for a drunkard. Maybe he wasn't drinking as I'd presumed. Better that he was not drunk at all, so that he might be hale enough to complete the task. His countenance reassured me.

"Don't you have servants for this? Why me?"

I picked at my rich red skirts. "In her anger, I'm not sure what she might say to the servants, and

I'd rather they not believe I've angered her. We discussed her future, and she is protesting being sent away to boarding school. Plus, if she's run off too far, the servants might not be able to find her, or she might not return with them. I need someone who can track her and bring her home."

He scratched the other side of his beard. Did the man have lice? I shuddered at the thought.

"So you want her to come home so you can send her away? That seems peculiar."

I screwed up my lips. Why did he put it *that* way? His statement made my skin crawl under my gown.

"Not like that. Royals are sent to boarding school all the time. It's time for her to go and she's being spoiled. I only have her best interests in mind."

"Sure you do. Her best interest is to send her away so you can have your husband to yourself? Why have her tracked to come home at all then?"

"Good sir!" I protested, stamping my foot. How dare he speak to his queen that way?

"George. My name is George."

I narrowed my eyes at him. "Fine. George. Watch your tone. I am your queen after all."

George bowed slightly, more mocking than respectful. I could not have been more disgusted and began to regret searching him out. If I didn't need his services so badly . . .

"Her father and I are only thinking of her future," I continued. "Her training as nobility is necessary and has been neglected."

"Hmm. It doesn't really seem like you want her back."

I leveled my steely eyes again, cutting his gaze with my own glare. First my mirror, now this man? What was wrong with everyone? Did I appear so black-hearted?

"We want her back. That's the whole reason I am sending you after her."

"Is it? I'm a huntsman, not a retriever. There's a difference, and you know it."

His tone held an edge that sent a shiver over my spine. He was so like my mirror, able to see into a deep, uncomfortable side of me I didn't want to admit existed. Into my iron heart that beat for no one. I lifted my chin at him.

"Yes, it is. Yet, huntsmen are trackers at their core, so you can track her. I don't know any other trackers. Can you do this? Make sure she returns?"

He bowed again. "Yes, my witch-queen. I can bring her to you."

I ground my teeth at how he addressed me, but he agreed to find her and that was all that I cared about.

"That's what I want to hear. She ran off behind the castle, into the King's forest. Normally she returns within the hour, but we've seen nothing of her all day. Can you track her from that?"

He nodded slightly, and the tight band constricting my chest loosened. I dug in my satchel, withdrew a silver coin, and pressed it into his palm.

"There will be more once she is returned."

I didn't quite trust him, yet what other choice did I have? Werner would be distraught at Sella's absence — he'd never recover if she didn't come home.

Then I spun in a swirl of serene cream and blue – a calming and a shocking contrast to the violent emotions churning inside me – and pulled myself into the carriage. Hans nickered at the horses into a canter, and I left the village without another look back.

I felt filthy.

Before the Magic Mirror

Chapter Twelve

When Werner returned that evening, I rushed to be the first to tell him the gut-wrenching news, that I'd spoken to Sella about her future, and she'd responded in her usual spoiled manner and ran off into the woods. His whole body broke when I told him she hadn't yet returned.

"What? But it's night! She's never stayed out at night!"

I enclosed his firm body in my arms and patted his back.

"I know. Perchance she lost her way. Don't fret, my love. I've already sent a man to track her down and return her to us. I will not let the jewel of your heart be lost."

Werner covered my hand with his broad one, and I noticed he suddenly looked older, worn out, with narrow strands of silver marking his shock of black hair. My poor husband, to have waited so long for me, only to then to have his daughter run off in a fit of anger. Would he never know pure joy? He deserved better.

"You are the gold that encompasses all in my heart, Adalee. What would I do without you?"

Strains of my spell danced in my head, and I forced myself not to shudder. Sella might well be here had it not been for me. Nevertheless, I pushed those thoughts from my head.

"Come, let's get you ready for bed. The man I sent won't rest until she's home, and it might be late before they return."

He placed his hand low on my back and escorted me up the stairs.

We had just changed into our bedclothes when a frantic pounding at the kitchen door frightened the maids. They squealed for a guard and then retrieved us.

Wrapping my bed robe around shoulders as we raced downstairs, I tried to calm the panicked maid. The wrought lass believed the devil himself banged at the door.

"Did you see the person at the door? He must have a reason to call on the keep this late!"

"A ferocious looking man, mum! And filthy —"

At this, I slowed our pace and raised a hand to the maid.

"Oh, Fran. He is of no account. Werner," I said as I spun to my dear husband, "the man, he's the one I sent after Sella! He must have found her!"

It had to be the reasons he was here. It *had* to be! What other reason could there be?

Werner's face alighted with happiness that sparkled in his eyes and made him look years younger. He grabbed my hand, and together we rushed to the kitchen door.

When Werner flung open the door, George stood there as I had expected, in all his gruff comportment, yet he was alone. Was Sella behind him? Was she elsewhere in the gardens, trying to avoid us? A sinking sensation filled my chest and made my knees tremble. Thoughts of my spell, of the wicked curse I'd chanted, rang in my head. Of the price that must always, *always* be paid. What had I wrought?

The dim torchlight from the kitchens cast him in a shadowy, diabolical glow, and he appeared even more the monster.

"Where is Sella?" I asked cautiously, leaning to peer behind him, searching for the girl. Had she managed to elude him?

George shook his head in a slow motion, and that binding pain in my chest clenched again, reaching to my neck. The air was painful to breathe in, piercing like knives in my throat. What had happened? Had he found her too late? Or not at all?

He held out a rough wooden box, shoving it at Werner's waist, and Werner took it without thought.

"It must have been an animal. I salvaged some of the, well . . ."

George's hard eyes remained lowered, the most significant sign of respect I'd seen on the man since I'd met him.

With a shaking hand, Werner opened the box and emitted a strangled cry. I snatched the box from him. Nestled inside was a bloody heart and locks of shiny black hair wrapped in a swath of Sella's red cape. I thrust the cursed token at George's face.

"What is this? What are you saying?" I whispered in a harsh, accusing voice. At this, George lifted his gaze, his hard eyes boring into mine.

"I didn't find her in time. She was deep in the woods, so far, and it appears she was attacked by an animal. Not much was left. I brought home what I could. I failed you, my queen. If you decide to withhold the remaining coin . . ."

An animal? I knew what animal killed Sella, and it wasn't one that lived in the wood. It was the one standing in front of me. I narrowed my gaze at George.

"No, no," Werner said in a low, achingly distraught voice. "Adalee, pay the man. He brought home what he could of my Sella."

Werner lifted the cursed box from my hands and turned away from the door. He set it on the table behind us, unable to tear his gaze from the gruesome gift, before starting for the stairwell. I focused my attention onto the man who filled the doorway. His rank odor attacked my nose, and I had to hold my breath and use a low voice as I spoke to him so my husband didn't hear. I yet eyed him — something of his story didn't ring true, but I couldn't put my finger on it. Why had he only brought home that little bit? Surely more was left of Sella if she'd been attacked, no matter the animal. A pang of regret fluttered in my stomach for ever involving this rough man. Mayhap I'd ask my mirror about George and his actions later.

"I shall retrieve your coin," I told him curtly. "But you must promise me, George. It was an animal that committed this foul deed, correct? Not you."

He had the good sense to look affronted, placing a splayed hand on his chest. I'll grant him credit — if he *had* slain Sella, he had the good sense to clean up a bit before bringing the awful reminder of Sella to our door. I saw not a bit of blood on the man. His hands, while still marked with dirt and grime, were free of any blood.

"I only did what I thought you'd have wanted me to do."

"That's not an answer, George."

"It's the only answer I have, milady."

His eyes held knowledge of something more, something darker. We stared at each other for the space of several heartbeats, and Simon's words about my stark honesty echoed painfully in my head. Not so honest anymore. What had happened to me? What manner of evil witch had I become?

"Wait here. I'll send a maid with your coin. Then our business is concluded. You will never speak of this, and I never want to see you again. Not here, not in town, never. Or I will curse the day you were born."

He bowed slightly, his face unencumbered by his dark work or my threat.

"Yes, milady."

That night, I held my husband as he sobbed his despair into my neck. Deep, slobbering sobs that wracked his entire body. My poor husband, who had suffered so much loss as of late. I feared losing Sella would break him. Even as much as I hated lying to him about my involvement, I'd continue to do it until the day I died. Or the day *he* did. He'd lost so much already, I'd not risk my love or my future with Werner. Not after waiting so long for him.

We'd both suffered enough.

"At least I have you, my love. You are my everything now," Werner sobbed.

And I was.

As much as I should have been dismayed at his grief and at the harrowing events of the day, his words made my sore heart throb with emotion, with joy. That same joy I would strive to bring to my husband as soon as he recovered from his mourning. It was now time for Werner and me, for us to make up for all the time we'd lost.

That night, I had to figure out how to start building our lives without Sella. And though a moue of sadness welled inside me for my husband, I was also a bit relieved that I'd never have to see the girl again. Her time of causing strife in my world was at an end. My mirror had terrifyingly spoke the truth.

As a result of my tampering with black magic, all the love and care in my heart had been destroyed — my price for those spells. Even for Werner, it seemed. I loved him in a way where I was more pleased that he belonged to me and no other, in the way that I was queen and living the life I was always supposed to live. It was a type of love, I guess, and I pitied him the loss of his daughter. But the passionate, consuming love I'd felt for him as a young woman?

No, not that love anymore.

I could easily admit to myself that I didn't have a care for Sella's death at all, no matter the anguish Werner felt. Did that make me evil? Had I become the evil witch Grandmother feared when she first showed me her magic? Some might say yes. I might even say yes, but not Werner. He believed I did everything out of our love for each other, and I'd continue to live that lie, too.

I'd have to consult my mirror on the morrow to learn what I must do next for Werner and myself. Looking at Werner in all his heartbreak, I had the idea that I'd be spending more time in my new cellar here, concocting and spell casting to keep him at peace. I glanced over at my black hooded cape. It would get a lot more wear from this point on.

Perhaps a spell or enchantment to cure his aching heart — just as my grandmother created for me all those years ago. It worked well, that I can attest. Then we might get on with the process of forgetting Sella and living for each other here at the castle.

The next day, leaving Werner to sleep off his grief in our lush bed, I wrapped myself in my familiar, comforting cape and sauntered down to my cellar.

I yanked the black sheet off my mirror before I studied my books and jars, tracing their textures with my fingertip. What could I do? What spell, what potion, would be appropriate? I couldn't very well have him completely forget her — that was impossible. And inappropriate. And might raise questions. Sella was his daughter, and any mention of her would throw his manipulated brain into a spin. A bit of residual dust from my books collected on my fingertips, and I wiped it away.

But something had to work. I scratched at my head.

What would Grandmother do?

She had been unapologetically pragmatic when called for, and I had to be the same. I needed to set my feelings for Werner and our future from my mind and determine the best way to cure his aching heart, and that meant I had to behave as my grandmother had, pragmatically.

He loved Sella, but after we held her funeral, which would be in a few days according to Werner's solicitor who'd called on the castle that morning, he'd require something to distract him from her memory, something to heal the emptiness in his heart. I'd do everything I could as his beautiful, considerate wife, but I couldn't take the place of his daughter.

That worn, ancient book sat by itself on a shelf, the book that held most of my black magic spells that I tried unsuccessfully to avoid.

Don't do it, my better sense told me.

I knew I shouldn't, not again, but I was desperate. I didn't even bother to look in my regular book. The situation with my poor Werner called for desperate measures, and this book called to me like a siren, encouraging me to use it.

I reached for the high shelf and grasped the leather-bound book. The list of recipes for spells and potions danced before my tired eyes and vibrated against my fingertips. Yesterday had been so long, so trying, and it carried over into the new morning. I must have looked a fright. Yet, when Werner woke later in the day, I wanted his heart to already be mending. So, no rest for the wicked.

Many of the potions called for complete memory loss, which wasn't going to work. He needed to retain some memories so as not to arouse suspicions about me. Then my finger landed on the entry for *Hardened Heart*, and I stopped, flipping the pages to that spell.

It was the opposite of a white magic love spell, but as my eyes scanned the recipe, I didn't notice anything too problematic or too dark. The object of the hardened heart was already dead —

what damaging effect could the potion have? Make *my* hearted more hardened? Hah. We were far past that point.

I'd need an apple, and a mix of my herbals, a black candle, and the enchantment. My mirror glimmered in the corner of the room. Uncovered, the face in the mirror came to life on its own.

"The magic has a price, my Queen," it cautioned. I shifted my eyes to my work, crushing herbs and an eggshell in a bone bowl.

"The object of the spell is gone. The price has already been paid," I lectured as I moved easily around the tight quarters of my cellar.

"Not the cost you think, my Queen," it continued, but I ignored it. I didn't need any more of my mirror's enigmatic statements right now.

With one hand, I tossed the sheet back over my mirror. It'd said far too much already, and I knew what I needed to do for my Werner.

The hardened heart wouldn't eliminate the memory of Sella, only the painful emotions tied to her passing. I'd give him the apple after her funeral — he must appear distraught for those who attended the funeral, put on his sobbing show. But after that, he'd eat the fruit and regain the vigor of his former self.

And Sella, well, we'd all mourn for a bit, but then she'd fade into the past until she was nothing but a distant memory, and Werner and I could begin to build our life, our own family together.

At the funeral, I cast my saddened glance to my husband as I touched the apple wrapped in cheesecloth in my pocket. Tonight we'd mourn, but starting tomorrow, Werner and I would begin anew. The apple was my assurance for that. I could hardly wait to have the relationship with Werner denied to me for so long.

I'd checked my appearance in my magic mirror before joining my husband, and the mirror vowed that I was yet the most beautiful in the land. It tried to caution me of the potion I had cast on the apple, of the cost, but I threw the cloth over it again, disregarding its warning. I was more than ready to give Werner his apple and the potion with it, and eliminate all our encumbrances once and for all.

"Here, my love." I held out the apple as we entered our chambers that night. I'd hung my formal gray cape on its hook and turned to gaze at him lovingly. "You didn't eat much today. I promise you, if you eat this, you'll feel so much better."

I knew I could count on my Werner. He trusted me so implicitly, loved me so much that he'd do anything I asked. He lifted the crimson apple from my palm and bit deeply, apple juice staining his lips as he chewed obediently. I bit my lip to hide the smile that wanted to curl against my cheek.

"Thank you, Adalee. You care for me so deeply. I'm so sorry I didn't see what was going on with Sella sooner. Maybe if I had sent her away to school before . . ."

I shushed him and stroked his lightly graying black hair. "Do not think on it. You're not to blame. She was just a girl and didn't know any better. We can pray for her soul and know she is in a better place. Finish eating your fruit."

He did as I bid, and as the pale core of the apple was exposed, his entire bearing shifted. No longer curved under sagging shoulders, Werner sat up straight. The dark shadows under his eyes had started to abate, and this time I let my slight grin peek through.

I'd known some potions to work quickly, effectively, but not like this.

"How are you feeling, my love?" I asked in a cloyingly sweet voice.

Werner set the remains of the fruit on the table next to him and stretched his long arms toward the ceiling. "So much better. And you're right about Sella. She was willful and didn't know any better. I had hoped for her to mature and wed her own prince, but with her willfulness, I lamented that would ever happen. I hate to say it, but mayhap all this was for the best."

I hadn't expected such cold words. A hardened heart for my Werner? My breath quickened — had it hardened against me?

"What do you mean, my love?" I asked as I moved to him, cupping the back of his head.

"I love her as my daughter, as my child, but her behavior as of late, it had been trying on everyone in the house. I'd have preferred she was away at school, of course, growing into the woman she should be, and I shall miss her beautiful face, her singing, her gracious attitude with the servants. Never think otherwise. Yet, mayhap she's in a better place now. She's with her mother, and that would make her happy. She will always be beautiful, and she's at a place where she's not so irritated by everything you or I said and did. That is what I must tell myself. Does that make me a loathsome father?"

My face buried into his neck as he spoke, so he couldn't see the smile I pressed against his skin.

Grandmother had always suggested her spells and potions were weak, nothing more than suggestion or putting our hopes and desires out to the universe. She believed her spells didn't have the power to make significant change. That the cost of black spells was far too high. But she'd been so wrong. So wrong. I had evidence of the power of my spells here in my arms. I had Werner, solved the problem of Sella, and managed to heal Werner's heart in minutes with a sweep of my wrist and a sound potion. He'd never know I had any hand in Sella's disappearance or death. And with my magic, it would stay that way.

My little secret to give Werner, and myself, our freedom.

Why had Grandmother treated her magic so lightly when she could have been a much more powerful witch, like me? Grandmother might have adhered to the epistles of white magic, but for me, I'd seen the benefit of black magic, so that's what I would use whenever I needed it.

I nodded my head against Werner as I listened to his precious heart beating in his chest.

"No, Werner. You could never be loathsome. That's a fine way to see it. We shall miss her, of course, but thinking of her in a better place, where she can be happy, play with her animals all day long, always be young and fair" — the words were like mud on my tongue — "is a good way for you to heal. You're still alive, after all, and you have so much life ahead of you."

Werner twisted his head so his full lips met mine. He tasted of sour apples and salt.

"So much life with you, my love. I know we shall have a long, happy life together."

My smile widened. He was right. This really was the start of our life together. I might be a wicked witch to some, but to Werner, I was his love. That was all that mattered to me.

And with Sella gone, what could possibly thwart the joy of our life? Now it was just Werner and I, forever.

With the power of my magic, both dark and bright now fully within me, I vowed joy would be all we'd know.

The End

Love what you read? Want more from Michelle? Click the image below to receive Gavin, the free Glen Highland Romance short ebook, free books, updates, and more in your inbox. Go here:

https://linktr.ee/mddalrympleauthor

Before the Magic Mirror

Look for *Before the Cursed Beast*,
coming early next year!

Before the Magic Mirror

Fairy Tale Notes

Snow White is an iconic fairy tale, one that's held up in the test of time. But the evil witch, I always wondered why was she so angry? Why did she use her magic like that? What made her so stuck on this idea of beauty. She was already a queen, what else did she want?

Those are the questions that try my mind every time I watch the movie or go on the Snow White ride at Disneyland.

I adore back stories of the different characters. And the evil witch was one where I wanted to see them outside of this one moment in time.

Those are the stories I love to read. It's like a sneak peek into a different world, one outside the story, delving into the characters in such a way as to make them richer, to make us care about them more.

I've always been a fan of the villains in our favorite fairy tales. I even owned a Disneyland sweatshirt at one point – a *Villains* sweatshirt. I wonder what happened to that?

So I just have to come up with a backstory for all these villains. Or the secondary character who just don't get their stories told.

I have an entire list of backstories I want to tell, so with any luck and a lot of time, I hope to give you an amazing selection of Before . . . books.

These stories are a move away from my usual historical romances. They are not as entrenched in history; they are a bit darker; and the don't necessarily end in the traditional Happily Ever After (gasp!). In this series, I tried to imagine, what would it be like for those villains before they were painted as a villain. Are they really as evil as they are shown in the princess story? What if I were in their shoes – what would I have done? Would the outcome have been any different? Could I have been painted as the villain then?

Oh, what might have happened! This series delves into those complex ideas, that maybe our villains aren't the villain we believe them to be.

I hope you enjoy these backstories as much as I do.

A Thank You to My Readers –

Thank you to my loyal readers – for you I am eternally grateful. Thank you for trying something a 'bit different from me.

To my kids and family, thank you for always supporting me. Even though writing takes me away from them, or I drive them nuts talking bookshop, they are my best cheerleaders. I couldn't do this without their support.

I also need to thank my Facebook groups and writing colleagues who provide guidance and advice when needed. We are a tight-knit group, and you all are so wonderful for helping me along this path.

My invaluable proofreader, Lizzie with Phoenix Book Promotion, who can read my writing in such a way to polish it beautifully, I also owe a huge thank you!

Finally, and just as eternally, I need to thank Michael, the man in my life who has been so supportive of my career shift to focus more on writing, and who makes a great sounding board for ideas. Thank you, babe, for putting up with this and for keeping me from being a villain and for giving me and the kids our own Happily Ever After.

Before the Magic Mirror

About the Author

Michelle Deerwester-Dalrymple is a professor of writing and an author. She started reading when she was 3 years old, writing when she was 4, and published her first poem at age 16. She has written articles and essays on a variety of topics, including several texts on writing for middle and high school students. She has written fifteen books under a variety of pen names and is also slowly working on a novel inspired by actual events. She lives in California with her family of seven.

Find Michelle on your favorite social media sites, all her books, and sign up for her newsletter here:
https://linktr.ee/mddalrympleauthor

Also by the Author:

<u>Historical Fevered Series – short and
steamy romance</u>
The Highlander's Scarred Heart
The Highlander's Legacy
The Highlander's Return
Her Knight's Second Chance
The Highlander's Vow
Her Outlaw Highlander
Her Knight's Christmas Gift

<u>As M. D. Dalrymple: Men in Uniform
Series</u>
Night Shift – Book 1
Day Shift – Book 2
Overtime – Book 3
Holiday Pay – Book 4
School Resource Officer -- Book 5
Holdover – Book 6 coming soon

<u>Campus Heat Series</u>
Charming – Book 1
Tempting – Book 2
Infatuated – Book 3
Craving – Book 4
Alluring – Book 5 -- coming soon